J.T. Fernie is the pen name of Moira Macfarlane. Her love of telling stories led her first into a career in teaching, then as HMI with the former Scottish Office Education Department. In 2001 she moved to Italy as British Consul in Florence, a post which she held for eight years until retiring for the first time. Three years later she took over as Acting Director of the British Institute of Florence for fourteen months.

Moira returned to Scotland in 2013 and lives in Haddington. She continues to travel widely and the books she writes draw on her experience of other countries and other cultures. *The Istanbul Gambit* is her second book, following the success of *The Istanbul Ring* published in January 2023.

J.T. Fernie

THE ISTANBUL GAMBIT

Best wishes
J.T. Fernie

AUSTIN MACAULEY PUBLISHERS®
LONDON * CAMBRIDGE * NEW YORK * SHARJAH

Copyright © J.T. Fernie 2025

The right of J.T. Fernie to be identified as author of this work has been asserted by the author in accordance with sections 77 and 78 of the Copyright, Designs and Patents Act 1988.

All rights reserved. No part of this publication may be reproduced, stored in a retrieval system, or transmitted in any form or by any means, electronic, mechanical, photocopying, recording, or otherwise, without the prior permission of the publishers.

Any person who commits any unauthorised act in relation to this publication may be liable to criminal prosecution and civil claims for damages.

This is a work of fiction. Names, characters, businesses, places, events, locales and incidents are either the products of the author's imagination or used in a fictitious manner. Any resemblance to actual persons, living or dead, or actual events is purely coincidental.

A CIP catalogue record for this title is available from the British Library.

ISBN 9781035881796 (Paperback)
ISBN 9781035881802 (ePub e-book)

www.austinmacauley.com

First Published 2025
Austin Macauley Publishers Ltd®
1 Canada Square
Canary Wharf
London
E14 5AA

I would like to thank the Marist Community LAVALA 200 for the privilege of spending a few days with them some years ago to experience at first hand the wonderful work they do in Syracuse to support unaccompanied refugee children, and to help them integrate into the society in which they find themselves. Most of all, I am deeply grateful to the children who told me their stories and whose voices need to be heard.

As ever, my thanks to the staff at Austin Macauley Publishers for their prompt acceptance of my second novel. I am grateful for the help and advice I have received from staff in the production department, and graphics department. Inspiration for this book came from many sources, from children who have known unbelievable hardship, and from the people who care for them. This book is infused with my love of Scotland, Italy and Istanbul.

Table of Contents

Principal Characters	11
Chapter 1: East Lothian, Scotland April 1997	13
Chapter 2: Siracusa (Siracuse), Sicily May 1996	20
Chapter 3: Leila Yousefi Sicily 1996	23
Chapter 4: The Search May-August 1996	33
Chapter 5: Flight from Sicily August 1996	44
Chapter 6: London August 1996	47
Chapter 7: Tasker Research Institute Dundee August 1996	57
Chapter 8: New Beginnings August 1996–April 1997	60
Chapter 9: Marmaris Nightclub, Edinburgh April 1997	65
Chapter 10: Disappearance April 1997	73
Chapter 11: An Identity Is Confirmed May 1997	75
Chapter 12: An Investigation Begins, Dundee May 1997	85

Chapter 13: The Aftermath of a Party, Edinburgh April 1997	96
Chapter 14: Soutra April 1997	102
Chapter 15: Fugitives April 1997	107
Chapter 16: Arrival in Bodrum, Türkiye	113
Chapter 17: Tayside Police Headquarters Dundee	128
Chapter 18: Cairo	133
Chapter 19: Bearsden, Glasgow May 1997	138
Chapter 20: Istanbul	141
Chapter 21: Escape from Captivity	144
Chapter 22: The Mosque Kitchen	148
Chapter 23: Orhan	160
Chapter 24: The Orlov Clinic Istanbul June 1997	166
Chapter 25: Ulrich	170
Chapter 26: Pera Palace Hotel, Istanbul June 1997	175
Chapter 27: The Boat to Lesbos	183
Chapter 28: Yasmin	200
Chapter 29: Cappadocia, Türkiye July 1997	204
Chapter 30: Azienda Ospedaliero-Universitario (University Hospital), Careggi, Florence 2008	207
Chapter 31: Amajgar's Story Florence 2008	212
Epilogue	216

Gambit-*an opening move in which a pawn is sacrificed to secure an advantage.*

On Loss

In my heart, there is a dark and vaulted well.
How crowded I am on the outside,
How deserted within.

Karin Karakasli
On Regret

And the most beautiful words ever spoken,
I have not yet said to you.

Nazim Hikmet
Voices of Lost Children

Night and stars streamed above us
where we lay buried—
along the road.

Bejan Matur

Principal Characters

In Scotland

DI George McAllister: Lothian and Borders Police
DI Graham Taylor: Tayside Police
John Arbuthnot: former superintendent: Lothian and Borders Police
Dr Hafez Yilmaz Yasmin Cilic: daughter of the owners of the *Izmir* restaurant, Dundee
Orhan Cilic: brother of Yasmin: owner of the *Marmaris* nightclub, Edinburgh
Professor Hugh Barnet: Tasker Research Institute, Dundee
Reg Manson: Gangland Boss: Glasgow
Ron Manson: Reg's younger son

In Sicily

Dr Daniele Antar: Cordari Clinic, Siracusa
Dr Hafez Yilmaz: Cordari Clinic, Siracusa
Commissario Del Santo: Questura (Police Headquarters), Siracusa
Leila Yousefi (Lara Menotti): a trafficked child
Raffaella and Corrado Menotti: Lara's foster parents, Palermo

In Istanbul

Commander Kadir Demercol: Istanbul Directorate of Police
Ayşe Demercol: charity patron and wife of Kadir
John Arbuthnot: former superintendent, Lothian and Borders Police
Anya Arbuthnot: former diplomat and wife of John
Yasmin Cilic

In Istanbul (continued)

Orhan Cilic: high profile wanted criminal
Ulrich McGurk: high profile wanted criminal

In Alexandria, Egypt

Dr Daniele Antar

In Florence, Italy

Dr Lara (Leila) Yousefi-Menotti
Raffaella and Corrado Menotti: Lara's foster parents
Amajgar Yousefi: father of Lara (Leila)

Chapter 1
East Lothian, Scotland
April 1997

Nothing in Miss Agnes Sim's tranquil, solitary life had prepared her for the constant anxiety of owning a puppy; or of the enormity of the task of protecting her from dangerous people, traffic, other dogs, sharp objects, slippery slopes, waterways and, worst of all, infections! She had already decided to be a little less judgemental of young women who failed to rein in boisterous children now that she had a better appreciation of what such responsibilities involved. Millie, her six-month-old cocker spaniel, was blissfully unaware that her unbridled energy and general joie de vie had an equally unbridled impact on her owner's nerves.

Miss Sim had to think long and hard about where and when to take Millie for walks to avoid hazards, in particular, the dangers posed by other dogs and people. Millie got overexcited if she met another dog and Miss Sim had to take her back to the vet every time this occurred to ensure that the excitement had not put a strain on her heart and that no canine infection had been transferred. The vet—an unsympathetic young woman—had been unhelpfully brusque on their last visit, dismissing her concerns in less time than it took the receptionist to make out her bill.

"You have a perfectly healthy dog, Miss Sim. She does not need to be cosseted," had been the terse diagnosis. It made Agnes wonder what on earth they taught at Edinburgh's Royal Dick Veterinary College these days.

To avoid the necessity of a return visit to the vet, she had taken to getting up at sunrise to walk along the beach at Seacliff when she could be sure that no one else would be about. It was therefore particularly annoying that, for three days in a row, a man with a golden Labrador had appeared just as she was leaving the beach. Fortunately, he had sensed that she did not want his dog to approach hers and kept his lab on a lead until the danger of a canine encounter was over, calling some sort of incomprehensible greeting as he passed. It sounded like, 'G'daiy, Ma'am.'

Rising even earlier the next morning to avoid a repeat encounter, Agnes and Millie set off from home in the half-light of early dawn. By the time they reached the beach, a rose-red glow tinged the sky over the eastern horizon, and the steel grey waters of the North Sea rolled into white-tipped breakers as they withdrew from the pale sand. They were alone. Millie began straining at the lead as usual, desperate to chase seagulls out into the sea where Agnes knew for sure she would drown when her attention was caught by something lying on the beach a little further along. In her excitement, Millie pulled the lead from Agnes's grasp and raced along the sand towards her target. To her horror, Agnes realised that it was probably a dead seal, crawling with maggots and riddled with who knew what deadly diseases.

Her desperate calls ignored, she set off at a run but after a few yards, had to slow down as many years had passed since she last took strenuous exercise of any sort. Millie was standing a little way off from the object and barking furiously. When she finally caught up with Millie, Agnes's heart was pounding as if it would burst through her chest. It was not until she had recovered slightly that she looked at what was lying in the sand and realised it was not a seal, but a fully clothed man. He was lying face down, head tilted slightly towards her revealing a sightless eye socket. Wet hair fell in strands across the exposed part of his face. His left arm lay at an odd angle, the jacket sleeve rolled back to reveal an expensive-looking watch.

The fact that he was wearing a suit and elegant leather shoes did not immediately strike Agnes as incongruous because she was in such a state of shock that nothing was registering. She did not even notice that Millie had stopped barking and was staring at her quizzically, waiting to see what her human was going to do about this unusual circumstance. At this precise moment, her human was shifting from foot to foot, wringing her hands and making strange whimpering noises.

Agnes had no idea what to do. She did not possess a mobile phone, having convinced herself that they were antisocial devices which allowed people to track you down at all hours of the day and night. The truth of the matter was that she feared she would not be able to work out how to use one—they seemed so complicated. And, of course, there was no one else around. Should she head for home and call the police? Or did she need to stand guard over the body until someone else appeared? It was all too much, and she was on the verge of tears when she saw salvation appear over the dunes with his dog. Seeing her frantic waving, he set off at a run, long, effortless strides bringing him to her side.

"Blaahdy hell!" Her saviour bent down to take a closer look at the body in a careful, professional sort of way. "Been dead for a while—and not exactly dressed for the beach!" It was only as he reached for his phone that Agnes took note of how smartly the dead man had been dressed before seawater had taken its toll on an expensive suit and shoes. This thought was immediately cancelled by a new horror. Millie, lead trailing in her wake, was chasing the lab in and out of the gently rolling waves as the tide receded.

The phone call to emergency services concluded; her saviour was in the process of saying that they should be careful not to disturb the site any more than they had already done when he realised that she wasn't listening.

"Millie!" Agnes screamed. "It's Millie! She's in the water!"

"I'll get her and take her lead off," he called as he ran towards the water, imagining, not unrealistically, that it was the trailing lead that worried the dog's anxious owner. When he realised that the removal of the lead had only added to the distress, he asked gently, "Is Millie the first dog you have owned?"

"Yes," she replied tersely, wondering what significance that could have in the face of the unfolding disaster.

"I am a veterinarian," he explained. "There is no need to be anxious. Spaniels are water dogs, and she will not go out of her depth. They are also sociable dogs, and they need to play. Our dogs will tire each other out eventually and that is going to make our wait for the emergency services a whole lot easier. We mustn't let the dogs near this poor man and if we try to hold them on leads, they will make a terrible mess of the scene."

"But isn't seawater harmful—full of infections?"

"Millie looks very healthy and will have a good immune system. Seawater will not harm her."

Agnes felt herself calming down as he talked to her about the mysterious life of dogs. Why weren't all veterinarians like this one? Keeping the distraction going, he introduced himself as Greg Hastie and told her that he had lived in Australia for the past twenty years but was presently looking after his elderly mother near North Berwick while his sister took a well-earned break. The lab belonged to his sister.

*

On what should have been his first day off in weeks, Detective Inspector George McAllister trudged wearily over the dunes and onto the beach. The call had come in as he sat down for breakfast, wrecking his plans for a game of golf and late lunch with friends. A twenty-five-mile drive through heavy rush-hour traffic had not improved his outlook on life. He was accompanied by two uniformed officers and DC Rajar Singh—one of the eager new recruits who had responded to the Scottish Government initiative to increase the number of police officers from ethnic minority backgrounds. He was a bright, cheerful young man, but this would be his first experience of a drowning and McAllister was far from sure he was prepared for the sight that awaited them.

A forensics team were on their way and McAllister hoped they would be able to wrap this case up quickly as an accidental drowning so that he could get back to the station and file his report. As his day off was already ruined, he might even have time to reduce the mountain of documents gathering dust in his in-tray. He had been passed over for promotion when his old boss, DCI John Arbuthnot had been promoted to acting superintendent, and the new DCI was firmly focused on prompt paperwork and rapid clear-up rates whatever the cost to her beleaguered team. Paperwork had never been George's strong point and his new boss's ill-concealed exasperation at George's slow, methodical approach to solving crimes was causing his blood pressure and stress level to rise along with a corresponding escalation in his consumption of whisky.

A few minutes later, George stared despondently at the body stretched out on the sand; all hope of a quick wrap-up gone. In George's experience, people who accidentally fell off boats or who attempted to commit suicide by drowning did not do so dressed in expensive suits, tailored shirts, and new Church shoes; nor for that matter, did they wear expensive watches. George groaned as he watched the duty pathologist, Simon Grewer, stumble towards them over the soft sand. Simon's default state of irascibility would not have been improved by being called out at dawn. True to form, he reminded all who should know better than ask for immediate answers—namely the police—that until he carried out a post-mortem, there was no way of knowing whether the lacerations to the head and the broken arm had been caused deliberately or accidentally, before or after death; or whether the skin discoloration was the result of prolonged immersion in water or something more sinister.

The man appeared to be fit, well-fed and in his thirties, but there had been no reports of a missing person or of a man overboard fitting the description. DC Singh's normally smooth brown skin had suddenly developed greenish undertones and to quell mounting nausea, he had turned away to 'assist' the uniformed officer who was taking statements from the two witnesses.

Dispatched by the police with thanks for their testimony and invited to North Berwick police station later in the day to sign statements, Agnes Sim and Greg Hastie made their way back to the car park. Millie was soaking wet, covered in sand and Agnes could not help noticing, deliriously happy. Greg asked if she would like to come back to his mother's house for a coffee and to let the dogs dry out in her garden. To her surprise, she accepted the offer gratefully—she was far from ready to be on her own after such a traumatic morning.

Chapter 2
Siracusa (Siracuse), Sicily
May 1996

It was already dusk when Dr Daniele Antar finished a long shift at the Cordari Clinic in the run-down Arsenale district of Siracusa. The clinic was based in a long-abandoned orphanage, and it was a charitable foundation providing free healthcare to migrants from war-torn parts of the former Yugoslavia and the Middle East. It had been an exhausting day, not helped by the increasing distraction of his colleague and friend, Hafez Yilmaz. They were the only doctors at the clinic, assisted by a small team of nurses, auxiliary staff and volunteers. Underfunded and understaffed, they struggled to meet the physical needs of their patients, let alone the psychological needs of people who had known terror, hardship and suffering on an unimaginable scale. Migrants, afraid of bringing themselves to the attention of the authorities, often left it very late to seek medical help and the increasing number of children presenting with long-untreated conditions placed additional demands on limited resources.

Daniele was the son of an Italian mother and Egyptian father and had spent a happy childhood in Sicily with frequent visits to his adoring grandparents in Alexandria. Hafez came from a family of doctors in Istanbul and he and Daniele had met at Istanbul University while Daniele was carrying out post-graduate research into the treatment of thalassaemia—research that now stood him in good stead given the number of Middle Eastern children presenting with the condition. It was while they were at university that they decided to work with refugees displaced by war or natural disasters. After five years on a steep learning curve with Médecins Sans Frontières in Eritrea, Daniele had responded to the call of a small Sicilian charity which had opened a clinic for migrants in his hometown.

Hafez had continued working at a field clinic in Eritrea with his Kenyan wife, Amara. A year later, Amara was dragged from her car, raped, and murdered along with her driver, by an Al Qaeda-inspired gang. Her crimes—running a clinic for women in a remote village; and being driven there by a man who was not her husband or close relative. Despite Hafez's dogged insistence over many months, local police failed to capture the perpetrators. To them, it was just one more death among many in a war-torn land. When Amara's case was summarily closed and the files archived, Hafez left Eritrea and joined Daniele in Sicily hoping to bury grief, anger, and frustration in work. This plan had been successful, up to a point—the point at which a young patient's story caused all his pent-up rage to resurface.

*

It took Daniele ten minutes by moped to reach the flat he shared with Hafez in upmarket Ortygia, unsure whether he hoped to find Hafez at home or not. He knew the time had come when he had to persuade Hafez to tell him what was troubling him, why he had become so secretive and why the frequent, unexplained absences from hospital and home. He knew it was a conversation they had to have—not least because Daniele couldn't continue to carry the additional workload—but he dreaded the inevitable confrontation. It would be difficult to get Hafez to admit to burn-out which seemed the most likely explanation, yet something had to be done for the sake of everyone involved.

The truth was that Hafez Yilmaz was caught in a vortex of obsession and terror.

It all began when a family friend had contacted the young doctor knowing that he was working with migrants in Sicily. Commander Kadir Demercol headed the Organised Crime Unit of the Istanbul Directorate of Police and was determined to close the routes for people traffickers plying their trade in human misery through Türkiye from war-torn Afghanistan and repressive regimes in Iraq and Iran. The onward trafficking routes he was most interested in were those destined for southern Italy via the Balkans or North Africa.

Over dinner in Istanbul, he had asked Hafez to pass on any relevant information he might pick up in casual conversation with migrants he was treating but had stressed that under *no circumstances* should he come to the attention of traffickers by asking direct questions. Not only had Hafez been asking direct questions but he had also been actively investigating the fate of some unaccompanied minors following a tip-off from a patient.

He had come to the attention of traffickers and was now completely out of his depth and very scared.

Chapter 3
Leila Yousefi
Sicily 1996

The patient, a 12-year-old girl, had been found in a ditch by an elderly priest returning home along a country road after a convivial evening with friends. Having consumed more wine that was consistent with the coping mechanism of his troublesome prostate—not to mention drink driving regulations—Father Andrea had stopped to relieve himself at a ditch running alongside the road. It was then that he saw the girl. At first, he thought she was dead, but on closer inspection, he realised that she was still breathing though barely conscious and haemorrhaging badly. Cursing the fact that he had left without his phone, he briefly contemplated driving home to call for help, then decided against it. Whoever had dumped her might well come back to finish off his task before the emergency services could reach her.

Even though Father Andrea was wiry and fit for his age, it took a super-human effort to pull her from the ditch and ease her into his car. She had put up a faint struggle when he grasped her under the arms but gave up almost immediately, perhaps soothed by his gentle words or simply lacking the strength to resist. From her skin colour and clothing, Father

Andrea guessed she was an immigrant and decided to take her to the Cordari Clinic. At least there, he knew, they would attend to her injuries first and ask questions later.

For four days, Hafez Yilmaz fought to keep her alive, fuelled by rage at whoever had forced himself and a pregnancy on a child whose slight body had barely reached puberty; and at whoever had thrown her out to die in a ditch when she became a liability, no longer a saleable commodity in their grim trade.

As the girl recovered, Hafez began to question her gently, all thought of Commander Demercol's warnings forgotten. Her name was Leila and she had fled Iraqi Kurdistan with her parents and some other people. Her father had paid a lot of money for the journey. Memories of the journey were a blur of endless days in the back of trucks, men shouting and moving them along with rifle butts, aching hunger, thirst, and terror. The nightmare had escalated in a filthy camp in North Africa where they were told to wait for the promised boat to take them to Europe. After several weeks of living in a makeshift tent, spending their last reserves of money to buy food, five armed thugs arrived and told her father in menacing terms that he needed to pay more money if he wanted the family to get on a boat.

Her father tried to explain that he had already paid for the whole journey, including a ferry passage to Europe and had no more money. He was rewarded with a rifle blow across his face. The men searched her parents' clothing and belongings at gunpoint and finding nothing of value, had taken Leila instead. Her last memory of the camp was hearing her parents' screams as they fought vainly against the traffickers who held them. She didn't know whether they were alive or dead. She was taken to a derelict building and injected with something. She woke to find herself in a frightening, dark place. All around she could hear the muffled sobbing of other girls and harsh voices telling them to be quiet. Her wrists and ankles were bound, and she had wet herself. For what seemed like an eternity, she was held in that grim prison. If she wanted food, she had to allow herself to be taken to a separate room where men 'did things to her'.

One night, she and the other girls were woken up roughly, shoved into a van and taken to a beach where they were forced onto a flimsy-looking boat at gunpoint. They were at sea for several terrifying days of searing thirst under a relentless sun. More than once she thought the boat would capsize. A little girl died and was thrown overboard. Leila prayed that some passing ship would save them. None did. She lost consciousness and the next thing she knew she was in the water. Her first thought was that she too had died and had been thrown overboard, then she realised that her feet could touch the bottom. Slowly, she pulled herself to her feet and struggled towards the shore. Behind her, she could hear the sound of the boat gradually fading into the distance as the traffickers abandoned their cargo in haste.

Around her, other girls were scrambling to their feet, their brief hopes of freedom dashed at the sight of more black-clad men on the otherwise deserted beach. They were rounded up and pushed hurriedly into a waiting lorry and taken on what seemed like a long journey—she thought more than an hour, maybe more than two. Night had fallen by the time the lorry stopped and the rear doors were opened by a man with a gun. He forced the girls out, threatening them not to make any noise as they stumbled over a stony courtyard. A run-down building loomed out of the darkness and the girls were pushed into a barn-like room and the door locked behind them.

Sometime later, thin mats were thrown in along with dry biscuits and water. They had been in this dark prison for four or five days, when Leila suddenly doubled up, a searing pain gripping her abdomen. To her horror, what seemed like a lake of blood appeared between her legs. One of the girls started shouting for help and a furious guard showed up, gun at the ready demanding silence. The girl pointed to Leila. The guard took one look and left. Soon he returned with two other men and dragged Leila out into a van. She had no recollection of that journey, or of how long it was before the door was flung open and she was rolled out into a ditch.

Hafez called the police as soon as Leila was conscious and well enough to respond to questions. Commissario Del Santo of the Serious Crimes Unit arrived shortly afterwards with an interpreter, questioned Leila for about 15 minutes and left asking her to let them know if she remembered anything else about her captors or where she had been held. On the way out of the building, Hafez asked the inspector what would happen next.

"Nothing more than we are already doing," had been the discouraging reply. "Leila hasn't given us enough to go on—traffickers operating out of North Africa, a stony beach with no houses or lights nearby, an abandoned farmhouse somewhere within a radius of 150 kilometres from where she was found, a van large enough to hold 12 girls—no make, no registration number, four men she had not seen clearly enough to recognise—men who might have been Italian—she wasn't sure. Apparently, only one of them spoke to the girls—in halting English. Not enough, I'm afraid. Have you any idea how many stony beaches and abandoned farm buildings there are within two-hour driving distance of the ditch where Father Andrea found her?"

"But surely you can't just let these monsters get away with kidnap, rape and murder. There must be something you can do to stop it!"

"Believe me," Del Santo replied tersely, "If I had anything to go on, I would happily incarcerate these bastards with minimum attention to the ideals of the Court of Human Rights! If Leila remembers a name or any other details, you have my number. I shall contact my colleagues in DIGOS* as they lead on organised crime. They may want to interview Leila, but only if she remembers something that might help to identify the traffickers or the location of the place where she landed, or the farm building where she was held. Take good care of Leila, Dr Yilmaz, and remind everyone who knows about her, that the official line is that she was found dead, and this is a murder inquiry.

"This is the only way to keep her safe and ensure that her traffickers don't come looking for her to silence her permanently. I cannot stress strongly enough that her survival must be kept secret. Social Services will find a safe place for her when she is ready to be discharged. And, a final word of warning, don't try any investigating on your own. These are ruthless men and, as you have seen, they do not hesitate to kill anyone who gets in their way."

*(Divisione Investigazioni Generali e Operazioni Speciali—General Investigation and Special Operations Division)

*

Ten days later, Leila stared in amazement at her reflection in a mirror. Her hair had been cut fashionably short and she was dressed in jeans, a white T-shirt and trainers—the first European clothes she had ever worn. They were less comfortable than the loose garments she was used to wearing, but she rather liked her new 'look'. Suddenly, tears welled up as she wondered what her parents would make of it all. A discreet knock on the door brought her back to the present. A lady from social services was waiting to take her to a family in a different town where they said she would be safe. She had to choose a new name and had selected 'Lara' from the list they had given her—it was the nearest she could find to her own name. She was to take the surname of the family who were going to look after her—Menotti.

She had wanted to use 'Yilmaz', the surname of the doctor who had saved her life, but the lady from social services was adamant she would be safer with an Italian name. Despite her brave new look, Leila was very frightened—she had no control over what was happening to her—it was like being in a kinder form of captivity. She needed to go to the bathroom again and she could see that the lady from social services was becoming impatient. When she came out, Dr Yilmaz was waiting for her, a beautifully wrapped present in his hands. "Can I open it now?" She asked. Dr Yilmaz smiled his assent leaving the lady from social services with no option but to accept a further delay.

Leila let out a whoop of delight and disbelief as a bright new Sony Walkman, earphones and a set of CDs emerged from the package. She flung her arms around Dr Yilmaz—a flood of Kurdish, Arabic, English words of thanks raining down on the man who had saved her life. Gently extricating himself from her embrace, Dr Yilmaz said, "Now you can be a real Italian teenager!"

Outside, an unmarked police car with two armed plainclothes officers waited for her and she climbed hesitantly into the back seat, followed by the lady from social services. As the car moved off, Lara turned to wave to Dr Yilmaz then froze. "What's the matter, Lara?" Her latest guardian asked.

"There's a motorbike with a man in black behind us!" Leila screamed.

"It's all right," the policeman in the passenger seat said reassuringly. "He is one of us and he is just making sure no one follows our car."

Leila sank back into her seat, still trembling. She had forgotten to mention to the police that she had heard motorbikes arriving at the farm and once, when the barn door was briefly opened, she had seen black-clad riders outside. She wondered if she should have mentioned it.

*

Sitting at his large, polished desk in the ancient palazzo that served as Carabinieri headquarters, Colonello Francesco Grüber listened as the young doctor vented his frustration at the lack of progress being made by local police in tracking down Leila's traffickers. In normal circumstances, Grüber would not have agreed to a meeting which risked crossing the delicate boundaries of jurisdiction among Italy's several forces of law and order, but Dr Yilmaz was a colleague of a family friend and he had agreed to listen 'off the record'.

Grüber sighed deeply, "So, all we know is that this girl was trafficked from North Africa as a minor, taken to an abandoned farmhouse somewhere quite far from whichever part of the coast she landed at; left for dead in a ditch at an unknown distance from the farm and found by Father Andrea at midnight ten days ago."

"That's about it—not much to go on, I know."

"How did she know the farmhouse was abandoned if she arrived and left in the dark and was locked in a barn until she miscarried?"

"Leila said there were none of the normal sounds of a farm, no voices apart from those of her captors, no sound of tractors or farm machinery, no sound of livestock, no typical farmyard smells."

"Could it have been an abandoned factory rather than a farm?"

"Leila was sure it was a farm. There were old bales of straw lying around and animal stalls at one end of the building."

"Did she hear any other sounds which might narrow the search—for example, could she hear the sea, or passing traffic, church bells or planes taking off and landing?"

"Nothing that she could remember. She said the place was silent apart from the voices of the guards. The girls were not allowed to speak to each other."

"That could either suggest that there were people close by who might hear the chatter, or more likely, it was to suppress any growing sense of solidarity or rebellion among their captives. From what she has told you of distances, this farmhouse could be anywhere in the provinces of Siracusa, Ragusa, Caltanissetta, Catania or even Enna. Have you any idea how vast an area that is, or how many abandoned farm buildings there are likely to be across it?"

"That is the point local police have made. They say they simply do not have the manpower to search every abandoned building for miles around—not when resources are already stretched coping with an increasing tide of migrants on top of an already crippling workload. All they have been able to do is ask squad cars to check any abandoned farm they come across in the normal line of duty."

"I would not have been able to do any more based on the information Leila has given, but I will ask the helicopter division to be on the lookout for any suspicious activity when they are in the air for other purposes. From what you say, though, this group only move at night so the chance of seeing anything is remote. I wish there was more we could do. It is a brutal trade with tentacles stretching across the globe and no sooner do we identify and close down one route than another opens. We stop and arrest the 'mules', seldom the money men behind them. What will happen to Leila now?"

"The police believe that the best way to protect Leila is to convince the traffickers that she is dead. As you know, the media have reported this as a brutal murder and during a very convincing interview on Rai Uno, Father Andrea described his horror at finding the girl dead in a ditch. Social Services have found a place for her with foster parents in Palermo. They have altered her appearance, changed her name, and developed a new back history for her. Police have asked the Red Cross and the Red Crescent to find out if there is any trace of her family in the camps in North Africa or Lampedusa but hold out little hope on that score."

Grüber rose from his desk and moved towards the window, momentarily lost in thought.

"It seems that everything that can be done to keep Leila safe has been done, and that has to be the first priority. I will pass on the information you have given me to colleagues in DIGOS who investigate trafficking. I'm sorry I cannot offer any more help at this time. Please, give my best wishes to Daniele—our families have been friends for many years, and please—be very, very careful. These people are extremely dangerous and will not hesitate to kill anyone who threatens their activity."

Hafez rose to shake the colonel's hand, trying to shield his disappointment behind a wan smile. He had already told DIGOS everything he knew.

"Thank you for listening. It is more than frustrating to think that these traffickers may never be caught and brought to justice, but I accept there is little to go on and that the police must concentrate resources on where they can achieve most."

Hafez left the Carabinieri station determined not to let the matter drop, whatever the risk to himself. Amara, his adored wife, would have expected nothing less.

Chapter 4
The Search
May–August 1996

Studying a detailed map, Hafez worked out a network of routes leading from where Leila had been found across the provinces where the farmhouse might be located. There were three main possibilities, a coastal route, an inland route and a mountainous route and each, assuming a maximum journey time of two to three hours, broke into a myriad of spurs along the way. Leila had told him that the vehicle taking them from the beach to the farmhouse had not been travelling very fast and that it had swayed around a lot. This made the mountain route more likely than the main coast road or motorway.

He called Father Andrea and arranged to meet him at his church which stood sentinel, as it had for more than five hundred years, over the steep, winding road far below. In response to the unspoken question, Father Andrea admitted that only a few faithful souls, mainly elderly women, attended mass these days. The Diocese had made no secret of their intention to close the church as soon as Father Andrea was no longer able to carry out his duties.

As he had told the police, he had found Leila just above the Convent of Avola Vecchia on a quiet stretch of mountain road leading from Casibile to Canicattini. The friends with whom he had spent the evening said that night-time traffic on the normally quiet road past their house had increased in recent weeks. He had passed this information on to the police but did not think they had taken it very seriously. It was the starting point Hafez needed.

Leaving the clinic early to make the most of the daylight, Hafez spent his evenings exploring every narrow track and unmade road he came across as he made his way up the tortuous mountain road to Canicattini. Most led for miles over arid, stony ground, winding over rutted tracks up steep inclines before dropping sharply into dark, forbidding hollows. Apart from occasional tractor tracks, he encountered few signs of recent human activity or habitation. Towards the end of yet another unsuccessful foray, Hafez had begun to lose heart. Increasing awareness of the scale and challenge of the task he had set himself had brought greater understanding—what he had earlier dismissed as inertia on the part of the police, he now saw as their greater grasp of reality.

With daylight fading, he was about to turn back when he noticed a turn-off just ahead of him. Unlike the other unmade roads he had explored, this one looked as if the loose white stones on the surface had recently been graded. On closer inspection, he found shallow tyre tracks made by a large car or van, not the deeper indents of farm machinery. He decided to carry out one last search before heading home. Carefully positioning his wheels along one of the existing tyre tracks, he rode slowly up the hill. After about 400 metres, he rounded a corner and caught sight of a rooftop in a hollow about 200 metres further on. He immediately killed the engine, dismounted, and hid his Suzuki GSX 1200 as best he could behind a straggling rosemary bush.

Hafez stood for a while listening for sounds of activity. A short distance ahead, the narrow track dropped down steeply towards the building, but from his vantage point, he could not see over the prow of the hill. There was no soft verge along which he could walk without making a noise. The ground fell away precipitously on one side of the track and a treacherous bank of boulders flanked the other. There was nothing for it but to walk along the track, unable to deaden the sound of his feet crunching on the loose gravel. He resisted the temptation to stand and survey the scene at the prow of the hill but continued his descent until he could be sure that his body was not silhouetted against the sky—one of many survival tactics learned in Eritrea.

There were two buildings in the hollow. The first was a tumble-down two-storey building, more like a shepherd's summer hut than a farmhouse. It was open to the sky, a few blackened roof timbers testament to its final hours. A windowless outhouse stood a little way off and behind it, he could just make out the demarcation of what might once have been a kitchen garden. There were no vehicles parked outside and there was no sign of human activity. A rusted bike frame lay drunkenly against the outhouse wall and a patch of coarse grass had grown around the remains of what might once have been a plough.

Hafez made his way slowly down the narrow track, stopping every so often to listen for any sounds betraying a human presence. Reaching the farmhouse, he flattened himself against the wall beside a window frame and peered inside. As his eyes adjusted to the dimness of the interior, he could make out an old iron stove and some broken pieces of furniture strewn across a cracked tile floor. A thick layer of dust lay over everything, disturbed here and there by tiny animal footprints. A steep staircase led to the upper floor, broken slats indicating that it had been a long time since anyone had ventured up there.

Hafez crossed the overgrown courtyard leading to the outhouse and cautiously pushed the wooden door, looking around anxiously as it swung inwards creaking loudly on rusted hinges. Four hens made a wild dash for freedom, filling the air with irate squawks and a furious flapping of flightless wings. It took several minutes for Hafez's heart rate to resume its normal rhythm. He knew that if anyone within earshot had been unaware of his presence up to this point, he or she would be aware of it by now, but as minutes passed without incident, Hafez relaxed. He slipped cautiously into the barn. A strong smell assailed his nostrils—hen droppings and something else, something chemical he could not identify. The earthen floor was covered in straw and a great deal of evidence of the hens' long occupation. There were no bales of hay, no stalls for animals and there was no lock on the door. This was not the scene of Leila's captivity.

He thought he heard something as he made his way back to the doorway—sensed a presence outside. Cursing his own stupidity, he realised that the outhouse was a perfect trap. There was only one exit and nowhere to hide. All a potential assailant had to do was wait for him to make a move. Looking around in panic for something to use as a weapon, he found a broken axe handle—not much use if the other person had a gun, but better than bare hands. In his other hand, he took a broken brick from a pile of rubble in the corner, flattened himself against the wall beside the open door and threw the brick as far as he could across the courtyard hoping that the sound of its fall in the near dark would distract anyone outside. There was no reaction—no sound of breathing or movement. Perhaps he had just imagined the presence of someone else. Gingerly, he edged out of the doorway and into the courtyard. There was no one there and casting caution to the winds, he ran back up the track anxious to escape from the eerie hollow and its real or imagined ghosts before the last rays of light left the sky. His Suzuki was lying on its side. He had left it standing securely and someone had looked through his belongings in the lockbox, replacing the maps, gloves and bar of chocolate carefully, but not as he had left them.

He righted the bike and set off down the track at a reckless speed, skidding to a halt in a shower of gravel where the track joined the mountain road. Descending a steep dip, he caught the flash of distant headlights in his rear-view mirror and a quick, risky glance behind confirmed that a car was gradually gaining on him from further up the road. Had it come innocently from Canicattini or was it following him from the deserted farm? He wasn't about to wait to find out. Glad that a bike had the advantage over a car on a winding road, he accelerated glancing frequently at the rear-view mirror. At Cassibile, he joined the main road back to Siracusa merging thankfully into the concealing embrace of heavy Friday night traffic.

Back in the quieter streets of Ortygia, he took a circuitous route to his apartment to ensure he had shaken off any followers. While he was parking the Suzuki, Daniele's car drew up alongside.

"Hi, Daniele, you are late home this evening."

"I could say the same of you, but I have been working until now. We run a clinic, you know—or had you forgotten?"

Hafez looked down in embarrassment but chose to ignore the barb. "What happened—was there an emergency?"

Daniele sighed, "It was the Albanian man who came in yesterday."

"The man whose foot was crushed on a building site?"

"Yes. The infection has worsened, and we may need to amputate—if only he had come in several days ago when the accident happened."

"But they never do, do they? Too afraid of coming to the attention of the authorities until the pain is so bad they can't endure it any longer."

"Poor man, he cried when I said we might have to amputate his foot—begged us to give it more time to see if antibiotics will work. He knows that casual labour where no one asks to see papers is his only prospect of employment and there is not much call for an amputee on building sites in Siracusa—and even less so in Tirana I imagine."

"What have you done?"

"Given him the strongest dose of intravenous antibiotic and pain killer short of killing him outright. I have sent X-rays and photographs to Sergei Lavrenty at the main hospital—if the foot has to be amputated, better done by an orthopaedic surgeon than by a doctor whose only experience of amputation was in an Eritrean Field Hospital."

"What did the old Russian bear have to say?"

"That we should have consulted him days ago—though how he thinks we might have done that before we had even met the patient was not clear! He says he will come in at the end of his shift tomorrow."

"That will cost you at least one night of conspicuous vodka consumption!"

"My liver is already complaining at the prospect!"

It had been a relief to set aside recriminations and talk about work, but as they entered their apartment, an awkward silence fell and continued while they prepared pasta and ate.

Daniele was first to break the silence with the question Hafez had been dreading.

"Where have you been since you left the clinic? Your bike looks as if you had ridden it through a flour mill!"

"Oh, I took it for a spin up a white road."

"Hafez, if you are doing what I think you are doing, it has to stop right now! You are putting not just yourself at risk, but clinic staff and patients as well. People traffickers do not appreciate doctors poking noses into their business and are none too scrupulous about how they put a stop to it—you must leave this to the police."

"And what have the police done? —Precisely nothing as far as I can see. Besides, if I can just find the farmhouse, then the police will be forced to take some action."

"For God's sake, Hafez! For a start, we don't know what the police have or have not done and for all we know, your actions could be jeopardising an important undercover investigation. Society works best if we all stick to our own jobs. Things start to fall apart if we try to do other people's jobs as well. You are a doctor—a very good doctor. Leave policing to the police."

The following morning, they left separately for the clinic. Hafez knew Daniele was right but sensed that he had got close to finding the farmhouse. Close, would not be good enough to spur Commissario Del Santo into action though.

A nurse on the afternoon shift burst in as he was discussing a patient with Daniele.

"Doctor, you need to come now. Someone has slashed the tyres on your motorbike."

The tyres had been not so much slashed as ripped to shreds, and deep scores ran along both sides of the bodywork.

"Do you need any further convincing, Hafez? This is a serious warning."

"It's probably just the work of local tear-aways…"

"Local tear-aways wreck bikes by taking them on a joy ride that ends badly. They don't come into a hospital car park with their mother's kitchen knife and cut tyres to ribbons for the hell of it! This is a serious warning from someone whose warnings should be heeded. You need to phone Del Santo, and it might be best if you disappear for a few days! Better and safer for us all."

"Don't be ridiculous, Daniele. How would traffickers know where I work—I haven't been followed."

"You reckon!! I am not going to stand around and listen to this, Hafez. Phone Del Santo or I will, and then make yourself scarce."

Daniele strode into the clinic without looking back. Hafez stared after him, torn between duty towards Daniele and the clinic and his overpowering need to bring traffickers and rapists to justice—a need fuelled by the trauma of Amara's murder. He was sure he was close to finding the farmhouse. He had to make one more attempt to find it. The problem was the bike. It would be days before it would be back on the road. The insurance company would want to assess the damage before work could start on it, and it was a well-known fact that insurance companies do not like to rush things.

Taking his car would be a risk. It could not be easily hidden or take sharp bends at speed on a mountainous road, but he had no other option. As he entered the underground car park below his apartment, he had an uncomfortable sense of being watched, but there was no sign of a watcher in the street or in the almost empty car park. He drove out cautiously taking a circuitous route out of town in the hope of shaking off any followers.

The day before, he had noticed a dirt track leading up the hill behind the farmhouse but had not explored it as the light was fading and he had been spooked by the sense that someone was watching him. This time, he drove down the steep track he had walked the day before and parked between the farmhouse and the outbuilding hoping his car would not be seen by anyone looking down the main track. He made his way through the old kitchen garden and out through a rusted gate onto the track leading up the hill behind the house.

Fifteen minutes later, he was looking out over an expanse of coarse grass and scrub. In the distance, he could make out a large barn alongside a dilapidated two-storey farmhouse. A white van parked outside the house looked incongruously new. He was sure he had found the place where Leila had been kept but knew he couldn't risk getting any closer. A lookout would have spotted him immediately walking across the open space in front of the buildings. He hoped he had enough to convince Commissario Del Santo to mount a search.

He found his car undisturbed exactly where he had left it and there was no sign of anyone following him on his journey back. As he climbed the stairs from the car park to his apartment, attention focused on the call he was about to make to Commissario Del Santo, a black-clad figure leapt out in front of him knocking him backwards down a flight of steps. The man was on top of him before Hafez could get to his feet, fists raining down on him. The last thing he heard as he slipped into merciful unconsciousness was a threatening voice whispering, "Keep out of affairs which don't concern you, Doctor—next time you won't get up!"

He had no idea how long he lay there before he regained consciousness and began slowly to assess the damage. His head felt as if it was on fire, he was sure his nose was broken, and one eye was half shut. He could taste blood in his mouth and every small movement sent waves of searing pain through his torso—cracked ribs. After a while, he managed to stagger to his feet, and clutching the handrail, made his way slowly and painfully up to his apartment. It was dark inside. Daniele was asleep. He realised he must have lain on the stairs for several hours. The call to Del Santo would have to wait until morning. He took a handful of painkillers from the bathroom cupboard, studiously avoiding the mirror, and lay down fully clothed on his bed waiting for the pills to work their magic.

The following morning, he waited until he heard Daniele leaving before staggering into the bathroom to repair as best he could the physical damage of the previous evening's encounter. He called Commissario Del Santo whose reaction was predictably furious, albeit a fury tinged with considerable professional interest. Hafez was instructed to stay at home, answer the door to no one and switch his phone off in case his calls were being traced. Del Santo would call around later 'to have words with him'. This appointment would never materialise, and Hafez would never learn that a detachment of DIGOS officers had raided the farmhouse finding nothing but evidence of recent illegal occupancy and a hurried departure.

Hafez would never find out that Daniele was threatened and eventually forced to leave Siracusa to seek refuge in Alexandria, or that the clinic would be left in the hands of two new, inexperienced doctors and a bewildered team of staff.

Chapter 5
Flight from Sicily
August 1996

Later that morning, ignoring Del Santo's instructions, Hafez left the apartment and phoned Commander Kadir Demercol from a public call box. Kadir listened to what Hafez had to say in mounting alarm. He knew Hafez's history, he knew about Amara, he should have known that Hafez would not limit himself to a listening role but would become so incensed by what he heard from people who had been victims of criminal gangs that he would throw himself into trying to stop it.

As Hafez's tale unfolded, Kadir wondered how many hours of painstaking work by the Sicilian police had been compromised because of the young doctor's actions. He would have to make a very difficult phone call to his counterpart in Palermo, but first, he needed to get Hafez out of Sicily. If the traffickers were onto him, even Istanbul would be too dangerous. Thinking quickly, Kadir told him to get on the first available flight to London and to meet him the following evening at his club in St James. In the meantime, he would call his friend, retired British policeman John

Arbuthnot, to ask if he knew of anywhere Hafez could lie low for the foreseeable future.

Hafez made his way slowly and painfully back to his apartment, aware of curious glances at his stumbling gait and bruised face. Tourists thronged the streets and cafés of Ortygia, their carefree chatter and laughter at odds with the panic and desperation overwhelming him. He was afraid—very afraid. For what felt like a long time, he stood shaking in the entrance hall of the apartment block unable to decide whether to risk the lift or the stairs. Memories of the previous night's attack on the stairs battled with the fear of finding himself face-to-face with a killer as lift doors opened. Finally, he moved towards the stairs, climbing slowly and silently, hesitating before each turn until he was sure no one was waiting around the corner.

The sound of his key turning in the lock made him start in fear, sure that the noise would alert any waiting assailant. He began to open the door very cautiously before remembering scenes of doors being kicked fully open in TV dramas to flush out anyone hiding behind them. He kicked the door wide open. The apartment lay open before him, dust particles dancing in a shaft of sunlight streaming in through a window. There was no one there. He threw some clothes, toiletries, passport, wallet and professional papers into a bag and was about to leave when he remembered he was going to London. He returned to his bedroom to collect sweaters and a padded jacket. As instructed by Kadir, he removed the SIM card from his phone and flushed it down the lavatory, then wrote a brief apologetic note to Daniele, called a taxi from the house phone, and left.

Hafez didn't relax until the airport bus left the outskirts of Siracusa en route to Catania Airport, and only then did the harsh reality of his situation begin to dawn on him. He was leaving everything he had ever known, everyone he had ever loved, for an uncertain future in a strange land without a sponsoring charity to ease the way for him. This was a different kind of fear.

Chapter 6
London
August 1996

The flight to London passed uneventfully and he slept most of the way. As promised, there was a message from Kadir Demercol waiting for him at the information desk at Heathrow Airport. Lodgings had been found for him with a Mrs Edelstein in Golders Green, historically home to a large Jewish Community and now a thriving cosmopolitan London suburb. The journey by underground took almost as long as the flight from Catania and involved a confusing change of lines at King's Cross Station.

Hafez's spirits rose as he emerged into the sunlight at Golders Green Station. Mrs Edelstein lived at the end of a row of terraced houses in a quiet, tree-lined side street. The door was opened by a well-dressed woman of indeterminate age; a mass of improbably black curls framed a strong face softened by a welcoming smile. He was shown to a large, airy room on the second floor with a view over rooftops to parkland beyond. The room was simply furnished with a comfortable-looking bed, an armchair and a desk. His few belongings would be lost in a fitted wardrobe large enough to hold all the clothes he had ever possessed. Mrs Edelstein paused in the doorway, unsure what to say to her mysterious guest. As usual, in such circumstances, the police had made the booking with a small inducement to leave the other rooms free for the duration of a guest's stay. But the young doctor looked very different from the usual run of people who found refuge in her home, the battered women and terrified children, the anxious men and women under witness protection. This man had a gentle face marked by sadness. She was good at reading faces—she had to be in her line of work, but there was something else about her new guest—was it just anxiety? No, more than that, he looked lost.

She would keep conversation to practicalities:

"You have sole use of the bathroom next door—I don't have any other guests at the moment. I hope you will enjoy your stay. Let me know if you need anything. Supper will be at 7.30 p.m. in the dining room on the ground floor if that suits you. I'll leave you to settle in."

Hafez turned towards her, a gentle smile briefly erasing the signs of stress.

"This is all perfect, thank you, Mrs Edelstein."

"Rachel, please. Call me Rachel."

"Hafez," he replied.

On her way back to the kitchen, Rachel Edelstein couldn't help wondering what lay behind the young man's need to be safely housed. This was not typical behaviour for her. She had long since stopped thinking about the circumstances that brought people to her door. It was about self-preservation—she couldn't afford to dwell on the awful things that had happened to her guests or to become involved in their stories. That way madness surely lay. But something about the young man upstairs was threatening to break through her carefully constructed shell of kind indifference. One thing was sure; Dr Yilmaz had recently been the victim of a violent attack.

Hafez threw himself onto the bed and re-read the instructions Kadir Demercol had put together with the British policeman, John Arbuthnot. He was to buy a pay-as-you-go SIM card, not from an upmarket phone shop, but from one of the small shops near Kings Cross Station where he was unlikely to be asked for proof of identity or residence. He should then send a message to Kadir confirming his new number. His meeting with Kadir and John Arbuthnot was scheduled for the following evening at Kadir's club in Piccadilly. He would be shown to a private room where they would discuss Hafez's safety and immediate future before dining. It was then that an alarming thought struck him. A London club would have a strict dress code and he had brought nothing but T-shirts, jeans and training shoes—the standard 'dress code' for medics working in hot and dangerous places, but a guaranteed passport to rejection from any self-respecting gentlemen's club in London.

What time was it? What time did shops in the UK shut—it was already 4.45 p.m. He seemed to remember that Marks and Spencer sold menswear at reasonable prices—might there be a branch nearby? He cursed his own stupidity. Forgetting to bring formal clothes was about to prove a very costly mistake.

Taking the stairs two at a time, he found an astonished Rachel standing in the hallway and explained his dilemma to her.

"I might have a better idea than trailing all the way to the nearest branch of Marks and Spencer," she said. "The Cohen brothers are closing their menswear shop in Golders Green—they must be in their eighties by now and have no heirs interested in taking the business on. It is less than half a mile from here and you might be able to get what you are looking for at a really good price. They may still be open if you hurry."

Hafez ran and ten minutes later found himself outside a double-fronted shop with a discreet notice in the window advising customers that, with regret, a closing down sale was in progress. The door was locked but on impulse, he tried the bell and smiled as an old-fashioned jangle rang through the shop and out into the street. The door was opened almost immediately by an elderly man with a shock of white hair. He looked as if he had stepped off the set of an Edwardian costume drama. His beautifully cut suit was from a bygone era. An expensive silk tie flowed from a high, starched collar and fine leather shoes polished to a mirror-like shine completed the ensemble. He held out his hand.

"Nathaniel Cohen. Can I help you?"

"I was hoping to buy a suit, but I see you are closed—when might you be open again?"

"We are not closed, Sir. Come in. Meet my brother Shimon."

"Whom do I have the pleasure of serving?" asked a mirror-image of Nathaniel, rising to his feet from behind a large mahogany desk.

"Hafez Yilmaz. A pleasure to meet you," he replied, before launching into an explanation of his predicament. The brothers looked at each other in mounting concern.

"We have a few ready-to-wear suits left but they are mostly in sizes for more robust gentlemen," explained Shimon casting a professional eye over Hafez's slight frame.

"In normal times, we tailor suits to order, but you say you need something for tomorrow. Let me see…"

"What about that suit we have in the back shop, Shimon? The one the Spanish gentleman ordered last summer, but never called to collect? He is not likely to come back for it now."

"Of course, of course. I'll go and get it and let's see if it meets Mr Yilmaz's needs."

A few minutes later, Nathaniel reappeared carrying a pale grey suit. Hafez tried it on. The fit was almost perfect; the fabric was a beautiful wool and silk mix and Hafez groaned inwardly at the thought of what it was likely to cost. The brothers studied him carefully and Shimon made a swift adjustment to the shoulder seams of the jacket. Nathaniel cast a disapproving eye at Hafez's trainers and reappeared with a pair of Church shoes.

"Trousers simply do not hang properly without the correct footwear. Try these and we can see if any adjustment is needed to the leg length. We keep a range of shoes for gentlemen who come in wearing casual footwear."

Hafez was amazed to find that the shoes fitted perfectly. *Obviously, there is something to be said for putting yourself in the hands of a professional tailor if you can afford it,* he thought to himself.

"We can have the suit ready for you tomorrow morning, Sir," Shimon said.

"How much will it cost?" Hafez asked anxiously quickly calculating that he would have to add the cost of a shirt, tie and shoes to the total.

"Let's see…" Nathaniel and Shimon huddled over a large account book, immersed in a whispered discussion.

Finally, Shimon looked up and said, "Does £200 seem reasonable, if we throw in the shoes—which aren't new of course—plus a shirt and a tie?"

It was far less than Hafez had anticipated. "That would be perfect," he replied immediately, afraid that the brothers might think the better of it. "Do you accept MasterCard?"

A look of utter consternation crossed the brothers' faces and it was only then that Hafez noticed that there was no till on the mahogany desk, let alone a card machine. Hafez did a quick calculation. The maximum he could draw from a UK cash machine was £100 per day, so he could draw £100 immediately and another £100 the following morning. He had about £45 in his wallet which should cover the cost of a SIM card and transport by underground. (Earlier plans to go by taxi to the club would need to be discarded.) He just hoped it wouldn't rain as an umbrella featured among the many items he had forgotten to pack.

"Normally, we send an account to a gentleman's home address…or to his club if he prefers to keep the cost of his tailoring from his wife," Nathaniel added with a twinkle in his eye.

"I will be leaving London shortly and am not sure when an account might reach me, so would a cash payment be acceptable?"

The brothers digested this novel proposal and agreed that a cash payment would be acceptable in the circumstances—these being the imminent closure of their business and their customer's transient state.

Hafez almost skipped out of the shop, delighted with his purchase. He would need to find some gainful employment soon and prospective employers were likely to view a T-shirt and jeans in much the same way as a major-domo at the door of a London club.

*

"Dr Yilmaz—I have an appointment with Commander Demercol."

The doorman stared doubtfully at the incongruous vision before him. An elegantly attired young man with a face that looked as if it had been exposed to the fists of a world champion boxer. "A road accident," Hafez reassured him. "I am sorry to hear that, Sir," the doorman replied before checking the daily register of expected guests.

"The commander and his guest are waiting for you. First door on the right at the top of the staircase, Sir."

"Thank you." Hafez strode swiftly across the cathedral-like hall towards the sweeping staircase. Evening sunshine poured in from a vast cupola, dancing brightly among the crystals of a Venetian chandelier before casting glistening pools of light onto the marble floor. He resisted the urge to take the stairs two at a time in deference to the grandeur of his surroundings.

Kadir welcomed him into a small, book-lined room. Dark leather armchairs surrounded a carved marble fireplace. An ice bucket, glasses and an array of drinks were set out on a console table, and he noticed that a liberal measure of whisky had already been poured into two of the glasses. A fit-looking man in his early sixties rose from one of the armchairs. He was clean-shaven with a shock of iron-grey hair and his welcoming smile was reflected in amazingly blue eyes. His handshake was firm and warm.

"This is John Arbuthnot Hafez. We have worked together in the past and he is a good friend. I am hoping he can help us find a safe place for you until the heat dies down. However, let me get you a drink first and then we can look at options."

Hafez opted for a soft drink. He did occasionally enjoy a glass of wine, but he wanted to confront his future with all his wits about him. He was relieved that Kadir had chosen not to waste time remonstrating about the actions which had precipitated his flight to London. His folly had already been elaborated in detail on more than one occasion by Daniele and Commissario Del Santo.

"I don't believe it would be wise or safe for you to return to Istanbul right now. We are fairly certain that the trafficking you stumbled across is routed through Türkiye, via North Africa to Europe so you would be at as great a risk there as in Sicily. Daniele is to move to the house that belonged to his grandparents in Alexandria. We wanted him to leave immediately, but he refused to go until replacement doctors were found for the clinic. Meantime, he is living with his parents and the Sicilian police have heightened security at the clinic and at his parents' home."

"Has Daniele been threatened?"

"Not so far, but the traffickers may want to find out how much you have told him, and as you know, they do not ask politely."

Hafez put his head in his hands as the full extent of the chaos he had caused in the lives of others began to dawn.

"Come on, lad, there is no point fretting over things that cannot be changed. We need to focus on solutions, now." Arbuthnot took a thoughtful sip of whisky before continuing. "Our first thought was that our National Health Service might find you a post as a doctor in a remote village in the north of Scotland. They are short of doctors in the Highlands. The problem with that idea is that a Highland GP is immediately a prominent figure in the community—on every dinner party list, featured in the local newspaper, their personal details a matter for public scrutiny. A good-looking young doctor who lost his wife while working in a war zone would set village gossip ablaze. On reflection, we think it would be better to hide you in plain sight and Kadir agrees."

How strange, Hafez thought, that his whole future was being determined by two men; one of them a total stranger, in a club in a foreign city. Until a few days ago, he had controlled his own destiny—or so he had believed. Was this what being a refugee was like? Of course, not—the future of refugees was not decided in the comfort of London clubs. Although he was the primary focus of it, he felt strangely detached from the conversation flowing around him. It was as if they were talking about someone else.

"John has a contact who leads a medical research team in the city of Dundee," Kadir said as John opened out a map of Scotland on the coffee table. "As far as we know, Dundee is not on the radar of the trafficking organisation you came across." Pointing to a small square on the east coast of the country, John continued, "The city has a population of around 250,000 and an attractive location overlooking the River Tay. Its University Hospital at Ninewells attracts students, medical staff, and researchers from all over the world so the arrival of a young, foreign doctor would not strike anyone as unusual.

"We think it would be an ideal place to hide you in plain sight. My friend, Professor Hugh Barnet, would be happy to take you on as a research assistant while you wait for your UK

National Health Service registration to come through—assuming you want to continue working as a doctor. There is a small apartment available within walking distance of the research institute."

Hafez suppressed a hysterical laugh. He was being banished to an unknown city in the frozen north—exiled for an indeterminate period of time until somebody decided that the coast was clear, and he could return to normal society and the warmth of the Mediterranean. It had all been organised without his involvement—job, accommodation, location. Everything! He knew he ought to feel grateful. Instead, he felt trapped, but it was his only option. Train tickets had been bought for the following day. John Arbuthnot would accompany him to his destination in Dundee. Kadir would return to Istanbul via Sicily where he would attempt to make peace with his counterpart in anti-trafficking.

Hafez allowed himself a glass of wine over dinner. His destiny was out of his hands.

Chapter 7
Tasker Research Institute, Dundee August 1996

He slept for the first part of the rail journey towards his uncertain future but woke with a start as the train pulled into Doncaster and John appeared clutching a bag containing sandwiches and a drink which John advised him would bear little resemblance to the coffee it professed but which was at least warm and wet. To Hafez's surprise, John proved to be excellent company and was happy to reminisce about Istanbul, a city John loved, and which Hafez missed more than words could tell. The views from the train became more dramatic as the journey progressed. John pointed out the magnificent Norman Cathedral and Castle as they passed through Durham and told him something of the turbulent history of the Borderlands.

Later, Hafez stared in awe at the rugged coastline of Scotland, the grey-blue sea stretching into mist-shrouded infinity and foaming waves crashing onto the cliffs below. Sheep—shorter and fatter than the sheep of the Mediterranean—grazed lazily on bright green cliff-top fields unperturbed by the noise of the intruding train. As they left

Edinburgh's Waverley Station, Hafez caught a brief glimpse of the majestic castle towering over a sheer rock face—an impregnable fortress which had repelled many invaders in the past, but whose survival now depended on a constant invasion of tourists. He stared in wonder at the impossibly long bridges spanning the Forth Estuary and wondered for a moment if he was approaching his destination on the far banks until John broke the reverie by telling him that they would arrive in Dundee in just under an hour. His spirits rose at the first sight of Dundee.

Perhaps his exile would be less arduous than he thought. As they crossed an even longer bridge than those he had seen on the Forth, he looked at the vast expanse of water glittering in the sunshine. The city rose from the shoreline up the steep slopes of a conical mound he would come to know as The Law.

They were met at Dundee Station by a large, avuncular man. A wild mop of grey hair framed his broad face, and his ruddy features were wreathed in a welcoming smile. His venerable tweed jacket had not kept pace with his expanding girth, revealing a checked woollen shirt and olive-green tie of similarly venerable vintage underneath. John and the newcomer embraced in the brief, self-conscious way of British men and John made the introductions.

"Hafez, this is Professor Hugh Barnet. You will be attached to his team at the Tasker Research Institute until your NHS registration comes through."

The professor's handshake was firm, and Hafez warmed to the man.

"Come now, lad, let's get you settled into your lodgings then we can head off to my house for lunch—I hope you won't mind the free-range children, dogs and general chaos which create the inevitable backdrop to dining chez Barnet. You must be hungry after your early start. This afternoon, I can take you to the institute to meet the research team and discuss our current project if you are not too tired."

Barnet's childhood had been spent more than a hundred miles further north and he had never lost the clear, melodious lilt of the Scottish Highlands. The accent was new to Hafez and not displeasing, but he had to concentrate to identify familiar words couched in different harmonies. What he had yet to discover was how gentle this accent was compared to those he would encounter over the coming weeks.

Chapter 8
New Beginnings
August 1996–April 1997

Over the next few weeks, Hafez's life gradually settled into a new rhythm. His second-floor flat in the Nethergate district was small but light and airy. It had recently been re-furbished and if the modern furniture looked a little out of place alongside the traditional Victorian fireplace and elaborate cornices, it was comfortable. Traffic noise generally subsided in the evenings except at weekends when partying students claimed the streets. Work as a research assistant was interesting rather than demanding and everyone assumed Hafez was simply killing time before his registration came through.

Hafez, himself, was far from sure he was ready to re-enter the pressurised fray of life on the wards of a busy hospital. He was experiencing severe flashbacks. Disturbing visions—of Amara's broken body, of a child found in a ditch, of assassins waiting in stairwells—invaded his sleep and during the day, he had to steel himself to climb the two flights of stairs to his apartment, listening with every step for sounds of a hostile presence.

Weekends were the most difficult and he dreaded the two long days in which he had nothing to do and no one to share the solitude. He enjoyed the occasional Sunday lunch at the Barnet's, enjoyed the chaos of children and dogs which mercifully impeded Hilary Barnet's gentle attempts to draw him into conversation about his past, but mostly he saw no one from Friday afternoon until Monday morning.

Richard, one of his colleagues had invited him to dinner at the large house in Broughty Ferry that he had inherited from his parents. He transpired to be an excellent cook and a convivial companion, but it quickly became clear that Richard had hopes of the relationship that Hafez could not fulfil. Much as he enjoyed Richard's company, evenings together could not become a regular event. It was Richard, however, who sourced a motorbike he could borrow, and exploring the beautiful countryside around Dundee began to take the edge off weekend loneliness.

It was on his return from one of these trips that he found a traditional Turkish restaurant in a rather down-at-heel area of the city. The owner and his wife came from Kemalpaşa near Izmir and were delighted to find a customer with whom they could relax and reminisce in Turkish, even if the customer did originate from that least Turkish of all Turkish cities, Istanbul. It was their daughter, Yasmin, who served at table. Unlike her self-effacing mother, Yasmin was a bustling, cheerful woman in her early twenties, rigorously attired in western clothing and sporting a broad Dundee accent.

The food was delicious—generous mezze with spicy hummus, aubergine slices in rich tomato sauce, falafel, olives glistening with oil and herbs and warm flatbread; an array of aromatic grilled meats followed and, for Hafez, the ultimate luxury, proper Turkish coffee served in a gleaming copper pot with a slice of baklava alongside. The Izmir restaurant became his destination of choice on all subsequent trips. The only discordant note in the otherwise relaxed, friendly atmosphere of the *Izmir* occurred on the mercifully rare occasions when the owner's son and friends rolled up in their C-class Mercedes. Orhan and his acolytes were large, intimidating men whose loud voices drowned out the conversation of other diners. Hafez was repelled by the domineering way in which Orhan addressed his parents and sister. Orhan lived in Edinburgh and the source of his ostentatious wealth was a matter of conjecture. It certainly did not emanate from his part share in a small restaurant in Dundee.

One Friday evening, Hafez relented and gave in to his colleagues' oft-repeated invitation to join them for drinks after work. Although Hafez enjoyed an occasional glass of wine with a meal, the Scottish passion for drinking to the point of oblivion mystified him. However, with heavy rain and high winds forecast for the whole weekend, anything seemed better than returning to his solitary flat. He sat beside Debbie, a bubbly lab assistant and let the conversation flow over him, marvelling at the rate at which she could consume vodka while he nursed a diet coke.

"Are you married, Hafez?" The question came out of the blue and in the minute it took him to respond, he became aware of silence around the table. The truth was that in his mind he was still married to Amara. Denying it would seem such a betrayal.

"I was," he said shortly, hoping the conversation would move on.

"Divorced?" Debbie was not about to give up her quest for information. Hafez was very good-looking after all and Richard had already confirmed that he wasn't gay, so his eligibility had to be checked out.

Hafez realised that all eyes were on the hand currently gripping his glass—to be precise, on the faint circle of paler skin on an otherwise olive-skinned finger. Seeing tears welling in Hafez's eyes, Richard broke in to defuse the situation.

"Come on, girls, Hafez is a widower; now leave the poor man alone."

Hafez rose abruptly and headed for the men's room, cutting short Debbie's delight at finding a handsome widower who might be persuaded to cast off grief along with his wedding ring.

"You'd better go after him, Richard," one of the other girls said.

"I think it's best we leave him alone. And, before you ask, I don't know what happened to his wife, but when he comes back, I suggest we change the subject."

Tears streamed down Hafez's face as he leant against a cubicle door for support. Nightmare images of Amara's broken body flashed before his eyes, drowning memories of all the happiness that had gone before. Not content with rape and murder, the thugs who had killed Amara had stolen her watch and wedding ring, leaving her sprawled half-naked on a dusty road, her driver knifed and kicked into a ditch as he sought to protect her. On the day of her funeral, Hafez had removed his own wedding ring and placed it on her finger before laying her to rest in the dry earth of Africa. The wedding ring that had left its pale shadow on his finger. The memory of the woman whose shadow haunted his waking hours and filled his sleep.

"You all right, mate?"—Hafez suddenly became aware of a burly, middle-aged man looking at him with concern. Mumbling a reply, Hafez fled. He was anything but all right.

Chapter 9
Marmaris Nightclub, Edinburgh
April 1997

Cold grey light filtered through thin curtains waking Hafez from troubled sleep next morning. Rain lashed the windows and on the pavement below, a woman struggled with a wind-tossed umbrella. With the day stretching out endlessly before him, he forced himself to brave the weather and head for a little Italian-owned café where they served excellent coffee. On his return, he found a letter from the National Health Service confirming his appointment as a registrar at Ninewells Hospital. Why did the thought of returning to front-line medicine make him so anxious? What was he doing in a cold, northern city surrounded by people who had shown him great kindness but who could not possibly understand the trauma he had experienced or the culture he came from?

Months had passed since his precipitous departure from the clinic in Siracusa—months in which he had done nothing apart from routine laboratory work which any minimally qualified trainee could have carried out. He could feel Amara's reproachful gaze—the gaze of a woman who had given her life to helping the sick in a war-torn country. What was wrong with him? Why was the thought of working in a modern, well-equipped hospital in a peaceful country suddenly so daunting?

To help fill the empty day, he decided to go for a late lunch at the *Izmir*. Yasmin was in a cheerful mood and despite himself he found his spirits lifting as she chatted enthusiastically about her impending 21st birthday party. It was to be held in a nightclub Orhan owned—well partially owned—in Edinburgh.

"Why don't you come?"

Sensing his reluctance, Yasmin rushed on, "It would make my day if you came. I could introduce you to all my friends. You have a great time. Please come!"

Hafez could think of few things worse than spending an evening at a nightclub owned—however partially—by Orhan, but faced with Yasmin's pleading, there was no option but to accept with as much grace as he could muster. He could spend a day exploring Edinburgh, drop into the birthday party for long enough to register his presence, then slip away early once the formalities were over. He owed Yasmin at least that for her friendship and for the sense of belonging he enjoyed at the *Izmir*.

It hadn't occurred to Hafez to ask about the dress code for the occasion, assuming it would be formal. He rose early that morning and packed a set of suitably elegant clothes—his 'London club' collection—in the panniers of his motorbike. He would find somewhere to change after a day of sightseeing. The journey to Edinburgh was uneventful with a brief stop at the village of South Queensferry to take photographs of the two spectacular bridges spanning the Forth. An old man at the pier reminisced about the golden days before the road bridge was built when ferries used to ply back and forth across the Firth. "And now there's talk of building a third bridge. Why can't people just enjoy living at a slower pace instead of flinging up new bridges and scarring the beautiful landscape with bigger and faster roads?"

Hafez, smiling his agreement, sauntered back to his motorbike hoping that he betrayed no signs of undue late twentieth-century haste. He left his bike at a car park near Edinburgh Castle, marvelling at the eye-watering charges for the privilege, and spent a pleasant two hours wandering around the ancient fortress, admiring the views over the city and out over the estuary towards the coast. Exiting the castle esplanade, Hafez made his way down a steep flight of steps to the Grassmarket with its cobbled, tree-lined streets and historic buildings, once home to the poor but now hosting restaurants and bars geared to the needs of weary tourists and stressed office workers. He stopped for a late lunch at Petit Paris, mercifully unaware that it was the last proper meal he would ever enjoy.

In the late afternoon, he made his way to Jenner's Department Store on Princes Street where a helpful assistant with an impenetrable accent, advised him on an appropriate perfume to give to a young woman. On his way back to collect his bike and change of clothes, he enjoyed a leisurely stroll through Edinburgh's New Town with its magnificent Georgian architecture and neatly laid out gardens. Leaving the tranquillity of Moray Place behind him, he re-emerged into the traffic and bustle of Queensferry Street and made his way towards Festival Square.

He had already identified the Sheraton Hotel as a good place to wash, change and while away a few hours until it was time to go to Yasmin's party. It was with some reluctance that at eight o'clock he closed his book and left the warmth of the hotel lounge to retrieve his bike from the car park. Orhan's club, *Marmaris,* was in the dark, run-down Cowgate area of the city and it was with considerable misgiving that he parked the bike on a side street hoping it would still be there on his return.

At the entrance, he was met by a wall of noise and an exuberant Yasmin. She looked amazing, although he was not quite sure what his mother would have said about the glittering dress moulded to cover only the most essential areas of her body, leaving the rest bare for all to admire. Flinging her arms around him, she dragged him off to meet some of her friends in the cavernous womb of the club where the air was redolent with the scents of alcohol, perfume, and costly narcotics. Most of the men were wearing designer jeans and brightly coloured shirts, an array of gold chains adorning necks and wrists. Aware of being hopelessly over-dressed compounded Hafez's mounting sense of discomfort.

Orhan was holding court in a corner, surrounded by leather-clad men none of whom appeared to be engaged in the party atmosphere swirling around them. As one after another of Yasmin's friends dragged him onto the dance floor, Hafez was surprised by the total absence of older relatives and children. In Türkiye or Sicily, all generations would have been present at such an event. The other thing he noticed was the absence of any indication that food might play a part in the festivities.

By 11 p.m., with the party in full swing, the effects of mood-changing substances of one sort or another evident in a deafening increase in noise and corresponding decrease in inhibition, Hafez slipped away quietly. Rounding the corner to retrieve his motorbike, he stopped abruptly. Orhan stood ahead of him, phone clasped to his ear and talking angrily to whoever was on the receiving end. Not wishing to be seen leaving the party early and reluctant to face accusations of eavesdropping from an irate Orhan, Hafez retreated into a doorway. The heated exchange was impossible to ignore.

Why the f--k has the boat come in at Cove? It was supposed to drop the cargo off just north of St Abb's!
...Captain freaked...Coastguard followed...from Eyemouth.

Hafez could only make out snatches of the response.

Cove Harbour is overlooked, you idiot—there are fishermen's cottages by the landing and a large house overlooking the beach. And even if the cargo is not seen landing, there are houses at the top of the cliff path. And the van is at St Abbs—it will take at least 20 minutes to get to Cove. What are you going to do with the cargo meantime?

The panicked voice on the other end of the call rose, *The dingy wasn't seen landing. The girls are in the Smugglers' Tunnel just above the beach and have been warned they will be killed if they make a noise.*

Hafez froze. He knew what he was hearing and the suppressed rage over the trafficking he had been unable to stop in Sicily threatened to overcome common sense. He was alone and unarmed. Orhan's henchmen were nearby. Biting back a challenge, he retreated further into the doorway. He had no illusions about what would happen to him if Orhan suspected he had overheard the conversation.

Wait in the tunnel—I'll send a message when the van arrives in Cove. You had better hope that an insomniac villager doesn't get suspicious about an unknown van passing through the village at midnight.

The van could always park at the Dunglass roundabout just outside the village.

Are you out of your mind? If an unknown van might raise suspicions, what do you think a column of girls tramping through the village calling for help might do?

Hafez held his breath as two of Orhan's henchmen approached.

What's wrong, Boss?

That fool of a trawlerman got it into his head that he was being followed by a coastguard vessel out of Eyemouth. He panicked, tried to outrun the coastguard and over-shot the landing north of St Abbs. The crew overpowered our man, ditched him and our cargo into a dingy off the coast at Cove, and then disappeared into the night.

F**k! Cove is the kind of village where they phone the police if they see a stray cat, let alone fourteen stray girls.

You think I don't know that!!

Boss, the road into the village is a dead end, it is a single track and passes within yards of the houses! The van will be heard. Could we not walk the cargo away from the village along the path at the top of the cliff and out by the outlying farmhouse—that way, there is just one household to deal with if the farmer wakes up, not a whole village outraged at losing its beauty sleep.

Brilliant idea! The only problem is that it is raining, the sky is black, not a trace of moonlight and the cliff path is exactly that. We would lose half our cargo over the cliff edge. We tell our man to hold the girls in the tunnel until 2 a.m. when we can be reasonably sure the villagers will be sound asleep, the fishermen still out at sea, and the farmers still in bed.

What about the van, Boss? It can't sit around in Cove until 2 a.m. without being noticed by someone.

I'll tell the driver to park somewhere inconspicuous between St Abbs and Cove until pick-up time. We'll have to go to Cove in case there is trouble. We can park on a quiet road outside the village and walk to the top of the cliff path where the van will wait. We are all wearing black so we shouldn't be seen. The first sign of trouble, we shoot. These girls are for the Manson Brothers in Glasgow. They dislike it when business deals go wrong! Get the others!

Hafez was still shaking as Orhan's large Audi pulled away from the kerb. He knew he should phone the police, but phoning the police in a foreign country was never easy and by the time he had told his story and the police acted, the girls would be long gone. He took a map from his bike and stood under a streetlamp to study it. Cove was about 45 miles south of Edinburgh on the A1. It should take him less than an hour at this time of time of night—the Audi would do it in less.

As he reached the outskirts of Edinburgh, Hafez wished he had taken the time to change into his leathers—he could already feel numbness creeping into his hands, but he decided not to stop. He had taken a few wrong turns on his way out of Edinburgh and a quick look at his watch showed him it was already 1 a.m. He still had 40 miles to go on the open road, find somewhere to hide his bike and find Orhan. Thirty-eight minutes later, he pulled off at a roundabout on the A1 and headed for Cove.

As Orhan's accomplice had said, the village stretched out along a narrow, single-track road. A motorbike going along that road in the middle of the night would wake half the village. He returned to the roundabout and took a secondary road towards Coldingham, but seeing nowhere to hide his bike, returned to the roundabout and took the smaller road leading to the Dunglass Estate. Almost at once, he spotted the Audi parked carelessly at the side of the road. He rode past it and parked his bike further on in a clump of trees.

Walking back towards the village, he regretted again not changing into his leathers. His white shirt and light suit were all too visible in the surrounding dark.

Chapter 10
Disappearance
April 1997

The narrow, single-track road into the village of Cove followed a line of neat houses, taking a sharp bend to the right as it approached the cliff edge. Hafez was acutely aware that he was an incongruous figure to be found walking along this quiet village street in the dead of night and like the traffickers, hoped that no insomniac dog walker or early-rising fisherman would emerge out of the darkness to accost him. After about 400 metres, both the village and road came to a dead end at the entrance to a cliff-top field. To his left, he could just make out a steep track leading downwards towards the shore—presumably, the track to the harbour mentioned in the call he had overheard between Orhan and his accomplice, but he realised that to attempt to go down the track would be suicidal.

The rough track was unlit and cut into the cliff edge offering nowhere to hide if he encountered trouble on his way down. The silence around him was broken only by the sound of waves washing up against the cliffs and the occasional call of a seabird engaged in some nocturnal fishing. On the far side of the bay, the velvet darkness of the night was lacerated by the bright lights of a massive power station. A sudden sensation of movement made him start but it was only a well-fed cat sauntering past in search of a midnight snack. Shortly afterwards, the silence was broken by the unmistakable sound of a diesel engine gradually growing louder as it made its way into the village. A white van slowly emerged from the darkness and Hafez hid as best he could behind a low stone wall surrounding the field. The van crawled along the village street making as little noise as possible, although the anxious driver would have known that, however carefully driven, a diesel engine had the potential to wake half the village population, not least as it turned around in the village car park and reversed the last few metres to the cliff-top path.

The driver killed the engine and remained in the cab for a further fifteen minutes until he was sure that no lights had gone on in the surrounding houses, and no barking dogs had been let loose to investigate the noise. Intent on watching the cab door, Hafez failed to sense movement behind him. He felt the heavy blow to his head, sensed momentary flashes of bright light and heat followed by a wave of intense pain, then nothing.

Chapter 11
An Identity Is Confirmed
May 1997

"Anyone seen Hafez this morning?" The concern in Richard's voice stilled the usual Monday morning chatter in the lab.

"It's not like him to be late—I hope he is not unwell," Professor Barnet's voice echoed the concern in Richard's.

"Oh, come on, Boss! He probably had one too many over the weekend, or maybe he met a girl. He told me he was going to a party in Edinburgh on Saturday."

Debby's normally infectious optimism dissipated as Richard continued, "Hafez seemed very preoccupied on Friday. I called him on Saturday to check he was all right and he seemed ok—said he was in South Queensferry taking photos and going to a party that night. We arranged to meet on Sunday afternoon, but he didn't show up and his phone has gone dead. I called around by his flat this morning, but there was no response, and his bike isn't there."

"Come with me, Richard. I have the keys to his flat. We'd better check this out." Debby's voice followed them as they left the lab, "You can't go breaking into someone's flat just because they are late for work..." But the two men were already out of earshot.

"I sense you know more about Hafez's situation than the rest of the team, Richard."

"Only enough to know that he had some kind of breakdown after his wife's death and that working at the clinic in Sicily didn't help matters. I don't know any of the details—he prefers to talk about art and music, and I am happy to go along with that. He knows I would listen if he ever wanted to talk about his past, but he just clams up if I ask anything about Amara or about why he left Sicily to come here."

Nothing seemed out of place in Hafez's flat. His laptop lay on his desk alongside a letter from the NHS confirming his appointment as a registrar at Ninewells, and receipts from energy companies. A framed photograph of a young woman smiling at the camera in front of the Blue Mosque in Istanbul stood on the mantelpiece. A copy of William Dalrymple's book, *In Xanadu,* sat on the bedside table, a bookmark inserted about a third of the way through. The television and CD player were in place and kitchen cupboards told of a single man's existence—some coffee, tea, tinned soup, a few biscuits and two ready meals in the fridge. A cup, saucer and plate were stacked on the draining board. His few clothes were neatly stored in a wardrobe along with the small suitcase Professor Barnet remembered Hafez carrying on his arrival in Dundee. There was nothing to suggest that he had planned to be away for any length of time, and no sign of intrusion or disturbance...or of his phone or bike.

"I need to phone John Arbuthnot—he is a retired police officer and a friend of mine. It was John who arranged for Hafez to have some time out working with us."

Richard nodded quietly. He had always sensed there was more to Hafez's story than a simple case of burn-out and he feared for his friend. The 'party' puzzled him. If none of his colleagues knew anything about it, whose party was it and who had issued the invitation? Why hadn't he asked more? He knew the answer—Hafez had seemed reluctant to discuss it and Richard had not wished to antagonise him by prying. As a gay man, he had been reticent about saying anything that might seem to cross a line and jeopardise this important friendship. Who else did Hafez know in Dundee? *The Izmir,* of course! Why hadn't he thought of it before?

He had been there several times with Hafez, and it was clear he was on friendly terms with the owners, particularly with the daughter—what was her name? — Yolande? No, it was a Turkish name…Yasmin! Should he mention it to Professor Barnet? No, the sudden appearance in the *Izmir* of a large, tweed-clad professor asking questions in his rich bass voice would turn heads. One of the many endearing characteristics of the professor was that his larger-than-life presence tended to command attention wherever he went. Attention was the last thing the situation demanded. He would go for an early evening meal before the restaurant got busy. With any luck, they would remember him as a friend of Hafez and there would be a chance to have a seemingly innocuous chat with Yasmin.

A heavy atmosphere pervaded the almost empty restaurant and the elderly owner was the only member of the family to be seen. As Richard greeted him, a flicker of recognition was swiftly replaced by a stony gaze.

"What do you want?" Was the distinctly icy welcome.

"Just a table for one—I'm sorry, I don't have a reservation," replied Richard with all the charm he could muster. With some reluctance, the old man showed him to a table and placed a menu in front of him without a further word. "How is Yasmim?" Richard asked when he returned to take the order. "My friend Hafez and I always enjoyed chatting to her."

Order in hand, the old man turned away abruptly, "She's not here." Not what Richard had asked.

*

DI George McAllister sat slumped over his desk, his head in his hands. The pathology report had just come in. The mystery man had been dead when he entered the water some 36 to 48 hours before he washed up on Seacliff Beach. His body showed signs of wrist and ankle restraints and he had been badly beaten about the face and chest. The cause of death was given as blunt force trauma to the back of the head. He was described as of Mediterranean appearance with fine features, possibly Syrian, Iranian or Turkish, and he had been circumcised. His outer clothing and shoes were hand-made but the tailor was no longer in business, and Church shoes were available in exclusive shoe shops all over the world.

Earlier, the new DCI had torn strips off him and his team, asking how difficult it could be to identify a well-dressed individual who had thoughtlessly turned up dead on her patch pushing up the crime figures. Had he checked all the shipping in and around the Forth over the last few days? Did she have any idea how massive a task that was—his colleagues were working on it, but it would be days before they had contacted every vessel with a good reason to be in the area at the time. Besides, crews in the habit of throwing bodies overboard were unlikely to respond truthfully to police questioning!

Had they been in touch with the Coast Guard? Of course, they had, but a suspicious sighting off St Abb's Head on Saturday night had failed to live up to early promise. Had they checked tides and currents to identify where he might have entered the water? — Well, of course, they had, but the Forth Estuary was fickle and this had simply narrowed the search area to 'vast.' And finally, why were up-to-date reports not on her desk? Budgets and clear-up rates were the priority—this case had to be wound up swiftly and with minimum call on divisional resources.

As if in answer to a prayer, his phone rang. It was his old boss, John Arbuthnot. John said that he was in Dundee visiting a friend and planned to travel on to Edinburgh that evening. Was there any chance that George could meet him for a drink—he wanted to run something past him? Off the record for the time being. With an investigation going nowhere fast, a drink with John was exactly what George needed.

From a quiet table at the rear of The Canny Man, George watched John Arbuthnot approach with two pints of craft beer. As John settled at the table, George observed rather enviously that marriage and retirement clearly suited him. John smiled and said that marrying Anya was definitely one of his better decisions. He was less sure about recent events which were drawing him back out of retirement.

"Tell me more."

"I should start by saying this is all very much 'below the radar'. You remember Kadir Demercol, the Turkish policeman who worked with us on the Gibson case? Well, some months ago, Kadir asked if I could help hide a young Turkish doctor in plain sight. He had come to the attention of people smugglers in Sicily and needed to lie low for a while. I found him a placement at a medical research centre in Dundee, but he has gone missing. The last known sighting of him was at South Queensferry on Saturday morning and colleagues say he was going to a party in Edinburgh on Saturday night. George! Are you listening?"

"Yes, yes, carry on!" If John noticed the sudden urgency in the other man's tone, he let it pass.

"He didn't turn up for an appointment with a friend on Sunday and didn't appear at work the next day. There are no signs of a break-in at his flat although his motorbike is missing. It is all completely out of character. We have had a quiet word with our contact at Tayside Police headquarters and we have agreed it is too soon to risk going public in case it puts him in danger. At this stage, we cannot exclude the possibility that he has been identified and gone into hiding. As Edinburgh was his last known destination, we wondered if you could identify a few clubs that might have been the venue for a large party of young people last Saturday night and have a quiet word on our behalf."

"George, what's the matter?"

"Can you describe this man for me? — You see, the body of an unidentified man in his thirties was washed ashore at Seacliff Beach between Sunday night and early Monday morning. He was olive-skinned, slim, of medium height and well-dressed."

John's heart sank. "Can I see him?"

Leaving their drinks virtually untouched, they headed out to the pathology lab.

There was no mistake. It was Hafez, dashing John's flickering hope that he would look at the face of a stranger—would experience the guilty relief familiar to all who have been called to identify a body only to find they are looking at someone else's tragedy. This was his and Kadir's tragedy.

"Was drowning the cause of death?"

"No, blunt trauma to the back of his head—possibly, a blow by a heavy metal object but we are still waiting for results from forensics. The poor lad had been restrained and tortured prior to death though—you can still see lividity on his wrists and ankles where some sort of rigid cuff has been applied. Several of the marks on his face and hands are caused by cigarette burns, others are post-mortem and caused during his immersion in the sea. The pathologist reckons the severe damage to his left hand is the result of something like the butt of a gun being smashed into it and not, as we first thought, by hitting rocks near the shore."

Questions raced through John's mind. Was Hafez simply the victim of an act of mindless violence? Had he simply found himself in the wrong part of Edinburgh at the wrong time? That seemed unlikely given how he had died and where his body was found. Edinburgh's gangs usually dumped their victims in alleyways or derelict buildings if they bothered to hide them at all. Edinburgh's criminals did not leave expensive watches on the wrists of their victims. Was it possible that traffickers operating in the Mediterranean had managed to trace Hafez to a research laboratory in Scotland? Had he revealed his identity to someone with links to organised crime? Why, after all this time, would traffickers still consider him such a risk that it was worth seeking him out to silence him 1,500 miles away from their field of operation? Was there something Hafez knew that he hadn't divulged to Kadir or himself?

Nothing made sense but one thing was clear, whoever killed him was either driven by hatred or wanted to extract information from him, or both. Why else would he have been tied up and beaten savagely before death? And who would go to the trouble of taking him, dead or alive, out to the North Sea before disposing of his body? Hafez's murder bore all the hallmarks of a contract killing. But why?

Back at police headquarters, John made a difficult phone call to Kadir Demercol, his apology for waking the Turkish detective in the middle of the night brushed off given the seriousness of the situation. They pondered the same questions and came up with no answers. Kadir concluded the call saying that he would break the awful news to Hafez's parents first thing in the morning. As Hafez was a Turkish citizen, he would need to make a formal report to the Turkish authorities and get official permission to travel to Edinburgh 'to assist the Scottish police with their inquiries.' He would arrive in Edinburgh as soon as possible, in an officially approved, unofficial capacity.

Early next morning, DI McAllister faced the unenviable task of explaining to his superintendent and new DCI that her predecessor and a very senior Turkish detective would be unofficially assisting his team with the murder investigation. In the event, his superintendent had no difficulty with the proposal. He held former DCI Arbuthnot in high regard and had met Kadir Demercol during the Gibson murder case. Impressed by Demercol's acute intelligence, superb command of English—and the fact that he belonged to one of Türkiye's oldest aristocratic families, he had even invited him to lunch at Edinburgh's prestigious New Club. He would hate anyone to know, but he occasionally fantasised about how his life might have worked out if he had been born to Scottish nobility. The truth was, he came from a very different background. His father had been a coal miner in Fife until he lost his job and embraced alcohol during the Thatcher years.

Seeing the DCI's ill-concealed displeasure, he reminded both officers that personal or professional jealousies must not intrude in solving what was clearly an internationally sensitive case. He had already spoken to his counterpart at the Istanbul Directorate of Police and assured him of the Lothian and Borders Force's full cooperation. McAllister's DCI managed to contain her anger until they were out of the superintendent's earshot. "Just remember who is in charge of this investigation, and that I need to be kept fully briefed at all times. You had better get this right, George, or I'll throw the book at you! I am not happy about the involvement of Arbuthnot—you were always too close to him—or with this Turkish 'extra!' Arbuthnot does not know the difference between 'official' and 'unofficial.' Need I remind you of what he got up to in his 'unofficial' capacity in Istanbul four years ago? And, I dare say, his Turkish pal is no better!"

With that, she stormed off into her office, slamming the door behind her. McAllister returned to his own office. Surveying the jumble of unattended papers on his desk, he resisted the temptation to sweep the lot into the wastepaper basket. How had John Arbuthnot always managed to keep that desk so tidy? He was at a loss to know where to start with this case. Which of the many national and international strands to pursue first? Which line of inquiry would eventually reveal a motive for the murder? And which line of inquiry would lead to the arrest his DCI wanted by yesterday? He was a good detective, but this case was way out of his league.

Chapter 12
An Investigation Begins, Dundee May 1997

John Arbuthnot phoned a worried Professor Barnet to pass on the unwelcome news, letting the horrified silence at the other end of the line linger for a minute or two while the professor collected himself. Unable to answer any of the distressed professor's questions, John asked if he could arrange a meeting of the research team and anyone else at the university who knew Hafez for 2 p.m. that afternoon. He, DI McAllister, and DI Taylor from Tayside Police needed as much information as possible about whom Hafez knew, where he went and what he did in his spare time.

Back in what used to be his own office, Arbuthnot found McAllister staring despondently at his computer screen.

"What's the matter, George?"

"Borders Police have just found Hafez's motorbike—or to be exact, a local farm worker noticed it parked among bushes on a country road leading to the Dunglass Estate. When he noticed it was still there two days later, he thought it might have been stolen and reported it to the local police."

"Surely, that's good news, George."

"In a way it is, but I now have an investigation stretching from Istanbul via Sicily to Dundee, Edinburgh, and the Scottish Borders. I have no idea where to start! I am not any good at handling the politics of inter-police force relationships, my DCI is in a rage and distinctly uncooperative; there is no obvious motive; we don't know where Hafez was killed, and most of the forensic evidence was washed away in the North Sea. Apart from that, I suppose finding the motorbike is good news! But what was his bike doing 40 miles south of his last known sighting? Did Hafez ride it there, and if so, why; or was it stolen from wherever he parked it before going to a party somewhere in Edinburgh?"

"Let's take this one step at a time. This afternoon we can interview everyone who worked with Hafez in Dundee. Somebody must know something about this party he was supposed to have been invited to. At the same time, can you get some uniform officers to trawl likely party venues in the city centre? Hafez wasn't dressed for clubbing, so we should focus on upmarket venues first—larger hotels that might have held functions on Saturday night—then if that reveals nothing, we should move our attention to some of the night spots in the Cowgate area. We can't exclude the possibility that it was held in a private house of course, but let's hope for the best."

While McAllister arranged for a car to take them to Dundee, John made a quick phone call to his wife Anya. Kadir's flight was being redirected to Manchester Airport because of an incident at Heathrow. She was on her way to collect him and would drive him to Edinburgh. John couldn't resist smiling to himself—Anya's motivation was so wonderfully transparent. If there was an intriguing case underway, she would want to be in on the action, not to mention relishing the opportunity to enjoy travelling time with their much-loved friend.

The car journey to Dundee was tedious. Lashing rain and high winds reduced visibility and caused inevitable, frustrating delays at the Forth Bridge crossing. On the motorway, spray thrown up by lorries and by idiots overtaking at speeds which took no account of driving conditions tempted McAllister to reach for the blue light, a temptation he resisted as they had no time to deal with offending drivers. After what seemed like an age, the profile of Ninewells Hospital on the outskirts of Dundee loomed on the horizon. Pulling up outside the research centre, they made a dash for the entry and found DI Taylor waiting for them at the reception desk.

"You've chosen a right awful day for traipsing up to Dundee," he said with a wry smile at the sight of their dripping raincoats, "but from what I hear about the death of that poor lad, there's no time to waste. I've got some CCTV footage of Hafez, captured on the days before he died—it's not much, but it might help establish where he went and who he was seeing. We can look at it back at the station once you have finished interviewing his colleagues."

That was more than John had hoped for and he was grateful for the unexpected assistance.

At that moment, an anxious Professor Barnet was hurrying towards the reception desk; all signs of his usual bonhomie gone. His face was lined with fatigue and his normally bright eyes told of stress and unshed tears. John's friend from carefree schooldays on the Black Isle had aged in the few months since they last met.

"I feel so responsible, John. I should have kept a closer watch on what Hafez was doing and who he was seeing, but I allowed myself to think he had settled down to life in Dundee and was making the best of it. He was well-liked by all of us here, though no one apart from Richard seems to have got close to him—much as at least one of the ladies might have liked to. They are all waiting for you upstairs."

"Don't blame yourself, Hugh. You did everything possible to help Hafez stay safe and settle down to a new way of life. From what Kadir has told me, Hafez has always been something of a loose cannon, and more so since his wife died. Tracking down child traffickers in Sicily became such an obsession that we had to extricate him from the danger he was in. Maybe we have underestimated the reach of the gangs he crossed. Or maybe he got himself entangled in some new obsession. We just don't know."

Professor Barnet led the way to the conference room where the research team were gathered in stunned silence. Two had clearly been crying, a delicate young man of about thirty and an attractive young woman whose thick tresses of blonde hair were losing the battle for confinement in the obligatory ponytail. John assumed these were the two colleagues Hugh Barnet had mentioned as being close to or wanting to be close to Hafez. As soon as introductions had been made, John took over the meeting before realising that he should have deferred to DI Taylor or McAllister.

Momentarily embarrassed, he looked over at his colleagues who both indicated that they were happy for him to lead. Some old habits die hard. John stressed to his listeners how important it was that they tell the police everything they knew about Hafez's friends, acquaintances, activities, and movements in the weeks leading up to his death. Had they noticed any recent changes in his behaviour? Were there any significant changes in his mood over recent days? Did they know of any acquaintances he had outside work and, most importantly, did they know anything about the party he was going to on the day he died? He added that if anyone preferred to speak to the police on their own, they could do so after the meeting. He could see they were all trying to be helpful but added little to what the police already knew.

Hafez had been well-liked and professionally respected. He was friendly but didn't socialise outside work. He didn't speak about himself or his reasons for being in Dundee, and any mention of his wife or what had happened to her was taboo. No one knew anything about the party or whose party it was. Debbie—the attractive blonde—had started crying again and Richard, the delicate-looking young man, indicated that he would like a word after the meeting. John thanked everyone for their help and called the meeting to a close.

Richard ushered the police into a small office and asked Hugh Barnet to join them. He told them that Hafez often visited the *Izmir,* a small Turkish restaurant in Lochee, an inner-city area of Victorian tenement housing and derelict mills. Richard had accompanied Hafez on several occasions and knew that Hafez liked the owner's bubbly daughter who served at table. She was the only real friend Hafez had outside work and she was the only person Richard could think of who might have invited Hafez to a party. The reason he had asked to speak to the police on his own was that Yasmin, the owner's daughter, also seemed to have disappeared.

Richard had gone to the restaurant in the hope of finding out where Hafez might be. He had found a gloomy, almost hostile atmosphere in the place, and unusually, Yasmin's father was serving the few occupied tables. He had barely acknowledged Richard as he set the menus down in front of him and when Richard asked where Yasmin was, the unhelpful response was, "She's not here." When Yasmin's father returned with his order, Richard asked when she might be back. "Not anytime soon," he replied.

Risking a further brush-off, Richard continued, "Have you seen my friend Hafez recently?"

This time, there had been no pretence at politeness. "I think you had better eat and leave. You are interfering in matters that do not concern you."

"I think these matters very much concern us," Hugh almost shouted. "We need to go to that restaurant right now and get some answers." John had a sudden vision of the reaction of owners and diners alike to the appearance of a large, raging, tweed-suited Scotsman invading the small, intimate space Richard had described. Noticing the alarmed expressions on the faces of colleagues in the grip of similar visions, John reassured Hugh that the police would follow up this lead at once, but that it was strictly a matter for the police. Hugh accepted his exclusion from further pursuit of the truth with considerable reluctance. He would like to have shaken Yasmin's father until some answers fell out of him.

McAllister gratefully accepted DI Taylor's offer to drive them to the *Izmir*. Driving in a strange city at rush hour and in pouring rain was no one's idea of fun.

"What do you know about this place, DI Taylor?"

"Graham, please! As far as I know, there has never been any trouble at the restaurant and neither the owner nor his daughter has form. There is a son who worries us though. He lives in Edinburgh and only visits the restaurant occasionally. You will no doubt have come across his name, George—Orhan Cilic. Has a large house in Barnton, drives flash cars, has a string of equally flash girlfriends, and there is no evidence of how he funds his lavish lifestyle. It certainly isn't from the meagre profits of a small restaurant owned by his parents."

"He is on our radar, Graham, but we have never been able to pin anything on him. He is part-owner of a nightclub in Edinburgh but as far as we know, it operates above board. That alone does not explain how Cilic affords his lifestyle. We suspect drugs and prostitution, but we have no hard evidence of his involvement in either."

The *Izmir* was a small double-fronted restaurant on the ground floor of a tenement building. Through the windows, John counted a dozen tables but the only customers were two workmen in high viz jackets. Attractive bronze lamps and posters of the seafront at Izmir, the Hellenic ruins at Ephesus and the nightscape of Istanbul softened the otherwise austere atmosphere. As John opened the door, a delicious smell of Turkish coffee mingled with spices wafted out, making him wish momentarily that he was there as a customer and not as a former policeman investigating a crime. A grey-haired man with a slight stoop approached from behind the highly polished counter. Lines of fatigue and worry coursed across his unsmiling face.

"Can I help you, gentlemen?" His English was strongly accented but seemed understandable enough.

DI Taylor introduced his two colleagues. "Is there somewhere quiet where we can talk, Mr Cilic?"

"I can't speak to you just now…I have customers and there is no one else to serve tables." The tremor in Cilic's voice was not lost on the policemen and the tense exchange now had the full attention of the two workmen.

"Mr Cilic, we can always continue this discussion at the police station if that is what you would prefer."

"I'll get my wife. Come through this way."

Cilic led the way through the spotless kitchen, stopping briefly to speak to his anxious wife who looked as if she were on the verge of tears. A doorway at the far side of the kitchen led into a tiny, windowless office with standing room only around three sides of an old metal desk. A rickety chair was squashed between the back wall and the desk whose surface was fully occupied by an ancient computer and equally venerable printer. A battered filing cabinet and flickering neon light added to the general impression of a struggle for survival. Whatever the source of Orhan Cilic's conspicuous wealth, this was not it. Looking at the exhausted, frightened man beside him, John felt a flicker of anger. The cost of just one of Cilic Junior's flashy possessions could have made all the difference to his parents' circumstances. DI Taylor's voice cut through John's momentary distraction.

"Where is your daughter, Mr Cilic?"

"What has that got to do with you?"

"Rather a lot, I'm afraid. We need to speak to Yasmin urgently. We are investigating the disappearance of one of your customers, Hafez Yilmaz, who hasn't been seen since he set off to go to a party in Edinburgh last Saturday—it *was* your daughter's party, wasn't it?"

Cilic gave an imperceptible nod.

John admired DI Taylor's skilful approach. Had he mentioned investigating a death, John was sure Cilic would have clammed up. Giving the impression that they knew the party was Yasmin's looked like paying off, Cilic assumed there was no point in denying it.

"Where was the party held, Mr Cilic?"

Cilic hesitated then, in the barest of whispers, "In my son's club."

"Which is?"

"The *Marmaris* in the Old Town."

"Just to be clear, this is the club owned by your son, Orhan Cilic?"

"Yes."

"Did you and your wife attend the party, Mr Cilic?"

"No, my wife and I stayed here to look after the restaurant—we don't have any other help apart from Yasmin."

"So, back to my original question, Mr Cilic—where is your daughter?"

"On holiday."

"On holiday where?"

"In Bodrum."

"In a hotel?"

"No…" Cilic, noticing DI Taylor's uncompromising stare, reluctantly added, "With family."

"Is Dr Yilmaz with her?"

"No! Orhan."

Ashen-faced, Cilic suddenly slumped to the floor, head buried in his hands. McAllister helped him gently back onto his feet, attempted unsuccessfully to release the rickety chair from its stranglehold between the desk and the wall, and settled for offering a glass of water and a steadying hand on his arm. Good cop.

"Sorry, sorry gentlemen, I…I don't know what came over me."

DI Taylor did not comment on the incident and resumed his questioning. Tough cop.

"So, you were saying, Yasmin is in Türkiye with Orhan. Does he often take his sister on impromptu holidays?"

"What kind of holidays…?"

"*Surprise* holidays."

"No. I don't know. I don't know what is happening. Orhan wouldn't tell me. Just said they would be away for a while. I haven't heard from them since."

"Thank you, Mr Cilic, that will be all for now. A Turkish colleague of ours may want to speak to you tomorrow, so please make sure you are available. Meantime, if you could give us an address and telephone number for your relatives in Bodrum, that would be very helpful."

"I have an address somewhere, but I don't have a telephone number."

"An address will do to start with. And if Yasmin gets in touch, please tell her to call this number. I cannot stress strongly enough how important it is that we speak to her. We don't think she has done anything wrong, but she may have vital information regarding the last known movements of Dr Yilmaz."

As they left the restaurant, Mr Cilic was on the point of collapse once more and John felt a moment's pity for the exhausted, frightened old man.

"We'll get Kadir's people to check out that address in Bodrum for us," John said as they made their way back to the police car, "but I hold out little hope of finding Yasmin there. Her father is probably being truthful about not knowing what her disappearance is all about, but he is clearly scared, and his priority will be to do whatever he can to keep her safe. And that might mean keeping her safe from us as well as safe from Orhan. I don't buy the story of not having a telephone number for his family in Bodrum and he is no doubt already alerting them to our interest."

Chapter 13
The Aftermath of a Party, Edinburgh April 1997

By the time their taxi arrived at the imposing gates to Orhan's secluded villa in Barnton in the early hours of Sunday morning, much of Yasmin's euphoria had evaporated. It had been a great party and she had been showered with lovely gifts, not least the beautiful perfume from Hafez. She had been disappointed when she discovered he had left without saying goodbye, but not really surprised. Wild parties were not really his thing; he didn't drink alcohol or use drugs, and he faced a long journey back to Dundee that night.

The real killjoy was Nadine, Orhan's girlfriend, her vociferously furious taxi companion—furious at Orhan's disappearance, furious at his lack of attention, furious at his lack of consideration, furious at his lack of appreciation, sick of his violent temper, sick of being surrounded by his unpleasant friends and sick of Orhan.

As the remotely controlled gates swung open to allow the taxi to advance up the short, tree-lined drive, Nadine fell silent and remained silent as they passed Ulrich, Orhan's burly henchman, at the front door. His voice echoed across the spacious hall as they discarded coats and high heels for someone else to pick up.

"Boss not with you?"

Neither woman felt the need to reply—the absence of Orhan being self-evident.

"I need a drink," Nadine announced pulling a bottle of Tattinger from the wine cooler. Reluctantly, Yasmin accepted a glass bracing herself for a further litany of Orhan's faults. Instead, all Nadine said was, "I'm leaving here tomorrow, leaving and never coming back!"

"He'll come after you, you know—he'll go ballistic if you leave. I've seen what happens to people he thinks have betrayed him or made him lose face. It would be safer if you let him end it—his relationships never last long."

"Wait until he causes me permanent injury or kills me, you mean?"

"Of course not, but where would you go? Where can you hide until he eventually forgets about you?"

"I'll think of something."

Nadine was not someone Yasmin found it easy to befriend. Nadine's was a world of glamorous clothes, Botox, breast enhancement, health spas, 'Hello' magazine and fashionable holiday resorts—all funded by the boyfriend of the moment—currently Orhan. Yasmin's world revolved around her parents and her host of long-standing friends; her determination to make a success of her parents' restaurant and protect them as far as she could from Orhan. Friend, or not, she was genuinely fearful for Nadine. Orhan would stop at nothing to find her, and when he did…

It was after 4 a.m. when Yasmin finally crawled into bed, drifting into fitful sleep as dawn broke.

She awoke with a start at the sound of angry voices in the hallway and saw to her surprise that it was already late afternoon. Suddenly her bedroom door burst open and Orhan barged into her room, his face contorted in rage.

"Where the fuck's Nadine? Ulrich said she came back with you last night, so where the hell is she!"

"How would I know; I have just woken up!"

"Don't get smart with me, you little slut! Ulrich said you and Nadine were up half the night drinking, so don't try to tell me you know nothing."

"Maybe she's just gone out for some fresh air if she is not in the house."

"Do you take me for a fool?" He said dragging her roughly out of bed.

"I can't tell you what I don't know…" Yasmin's words died in the air as Orhan struck her.

"You have lots to tell me, Yasmin, not just about Nadine, but about why that Turkish boyfriend of yours has been poking his nose into things that don't concern him! Get dressed—we are leaving."

Before she had a chance to ask what he meant about Hafez poking his nose into things that didn't concern him, Orhan stormed out of her room slamming the door behind him. The warm water of the shower eased her aching face but did nothing to still her shaking knees. She was very scared, not just for herself, but for Hafez and Nadine too. She had no way of knowing that it was already too late for Hafez. And what did Orhan mean by 'we're leaving?' Leaving for where? She had to be at the airport by 8 p.m. to meet her best friend for the late-night flight to Malaga—a birthday present from her father.

She dressed quickly and crept down the stairs to the main hall where she had left her passport, plane tickets, hotel reservations and euros on a desk beside her suitcase. To her horror, only the suitcase remained. All her travel documents and money had vanished, and it took little imagination to work out who had removed them. The main door was open, and Ulrich was already in the driver's seat of Orhan's car with the engine running. Orhan appeared carrying a large suitcase and dragged her by the arm to the waiting car, returning to collect her case from the hall.

"What's happening? Where are we going?" She demanded—angry that her voice betrayed fear.

"Shut up! You and your fucking Turkish boyfriend are the cause of all of this."

"But I have to be at Edinburgh Airport by 8 to meet Lucy."

"Oh, you'll be at an airport all right, but not for a jaunt to Malaga. You're coming with me!"

"But I…" a blow to the head silenced her as the car made its way to the Maybury roundabout and the M8 towards Glasgow.

The truth was, Orhan had to disappear as a matter of very considerable urgency. It wasn't simply because of a bungled consignment complicated by murder—a murder witnessed by fishermen whose loyalty to Orhan was only cash-deep. It wasn't simply about the outstanding payment for taking Orhan and his entourage out to sea to interrogate and dispose of Yilmaz. Despite their losses, he was confident that the captain and crew of *The Skua* would not wish to draw the attention of the police to their main source of income—fishing being simply a convenient cover for more profitable activity. Unless a member of the crew talked, it was unlikely that Hafez

Yilmaz's death could be traced back to him. No, the problem was much more serious.

The consignment of girls had been destined for Ronnie Manson—son of Reggie, one of Glasgow gangland's most notorious bosses. But Ronnie had refused to take the girls or pay for the consignment. He wasn't convinced that Hafez Yilmaz had been working on his own and he did not share Orhan's confidence that Yilmaz's death would never come to light. Landing the girls in a coastal village where any number of prying eyes might have seen them had been no part of the agreement. The deal was compromised, and he was calling it off. Ronnie was terrified of his father's reaction if he found out that he had been trafficking underage girls. Following a stroke, Reggie Manson might have stepped back from the day-to-day running of the family business, but he was still a force to be reckoned with. And Reggie had always espoused one unbreakable principle—the Mansons did not touch children. They did not deal in child trafficking, kidnapping children, or procuring underage kids for prostitution.

Reggie had no qualms about dealing in murder, illegal drugs, adult prostitution, adult kidnapping, money laundering, protection rackets or almost any other form of serious crime you could name. But NEVER kids! Orhan's bungled deal could lead to all sorts of complications, any one of which could come to Reggie's attention. The deal was off. It was up to Orhan to get rid of the girls quietly and permanently. In the event, Orhan's associates had baulked at killing the girls as instructed and had thrown them out of the van on a remote hillside near Soutra, hoping that it would be some time before they were found; if they were found, and if they survived a night out on the unforgiving hills. They had forgotten—if they ever knew—how early sheep farmers and their dogs take to the hills.

The cancelled deal meant that Orhan could not pay for the procurement of the girls in the Balkans, or for their illegal transportation by road and sea to Scotland. A lot of unpleasant people were looking for immediate settlement of debts for services rendered. Patience and understanding were not notable characteristics of Orhan's business associates. He had to disappear and as his sister might know more than was good for her, she would have to disappear too.

Chapter 14
Soutra April 1997

Dawn was breaking as Peter Jones, accompanied by Max his faithful sheepdog, left the warmth of home to check on his new lambs. The lambs had only been out on the hills for two weeks as there had been an unexpected cold snap at the end of April and the hillsides at Soutra caught every chill wind that was blowing. A light covering of dew sparkled in the early morning sunshine on what promised to be a fine Spring Day. Max trotted along at his master's heel, happy at the prospect of doing what he did best, restoring order to a disorderly flock of sheep. At six years old, Max was the best dog Peter had ever owned and the proud winner of several sheepdog trial rosettes. Peter was therefore astonished when Max suddenly shot off disappearing behind a low rise on the hillside and barking furiously.

Peter set off up the rise as fast as his legs would carry him, puzzled by the dog's behaviour and worried about what he might find. What he saw at the top of the rise left him speechless. Not a fox or a raptor as he had feared, but a huddle of terrified girls standing stock still staring at the dog. They looked about ten or eleven years old. His initial thought that this was a school party or group of Girl Guides who had got lost was quickly discarded as he took in the style of their dress and the deep olive colouring of their skin. When he began to move towards them, they clutched each other in fear and he stopped, holding out his arms in what he hoped was a gesture of peace.

"What are you doing here?" He asked, his question left hanging in the air.

"Where are you from?"—still no response.

Max had stopped barking and was looking quizzically at his master. Sheep were one thing, a flock of girls was another matter altogether.

Peter was at a loss. He couldn't leave them there—their light clothing and footwear were no match for a Scottish hillside, and they looked half-starved and frozen.

The question was how to get them to the farmhouse where his wife could look after them till the police, social services or whoever dealt with lost girls arrived. But they were obviously scared and made no move when he signalled to follow him. Seeing his master's difficulty, Max moved in to do what he did best—round up disorderly beings and herd them in whichever direction his master indicated. The girls were wary of the dog and as he circled around them in a low crouch, they moved in the direction intended with Peter walking ahead at a distance.

Peter's wife, Mary, stared in astonishment at the sight of her husband returning like the Pied Piper at the head of a group of girls. He paused at the front door when he realised that movement behind him had stopped as Max awaited instructions as to whether he had to herd his flock into the pen or the shed. Mary took charge of the situation, and the girls allowed the apron-clad, motherly figure to approach.

"Found them on top o' the hill—they dinnae speak English," Peter called out to her. Mary paid no attention but continued her slow walk towards the girls, a welcoming smile lighting up her kindly blue eyes. Making the internationally understood actions of eating and drinking, she encouraged the girls to follow her to the house. Two of the older girls made the first cautious move swiftly followed by the others, hunger and cold overcoming their fear.

In the warmth of the farmhouse kitchen, bread, cheese, eggs and tea were devoured at lightning speed.

"They poor lassies have been dumped by smugglers, mark my words," Mary announced in a voice full of anger and concern as she told Peter to phone the police. "And tell them no to come wi' their flashing lights and scary gear. They girls need women officers in civies and a social worker that kens whit she is doing."

"Wait a tick!" Peter wondered what she was going to do next. Mary disappeared into the living room returning with a large atlas opened at a map of Europe. Motioning to the two oldest girls to join her, she began pointing first to Albania and then to Montenegro. The girls shook their heads and one of them leant over and pointed to Romania. Mary let her finger hover over Bucharest and the girl again shook her head, pointing to Timişoara instead.

"And tell the police they'll need to bring a Romanian interpreter wi' them. They wee lassies are not leaving this house unless they understand what's to happen to them and are ok wi' that! So, tell them the interpreter needs to come *here* to speak to them. Now, off wi' ye—I've a pot of soup to make before they lassies get any thinner."

While Peter phoned the police, advising them to follow Mary's instructions to the letter if they didn't want to be met at the door by an elderly woman brandishing a shotgun, towels and soap were produced and the girls were shown where they could freshen up.

The sound of muffled tears drew Mary's attention to the smallest child who looked to be no more than seven or eight. Mary took her on her knee and began to sing softly one of the gentle lullabies of her native Isles. Before long, the little girl fell asleep, and Mary laid her on a sofa and covered her with a blanket. Next, she set about making a huge pot of soup for soon there would be police, social workers, interpreters, and most importantly, wee lassies to feed. Peter and Max took advantage of a lull in proceedings to check on the lambs.

The police arrived to find the girls sitting around a blazing fire in the living room devouring mugs of potato soup and sandwiches. As instructed, they had appeared in civilian clothes accompanied by two specialist social workers and a gentle young man from the Romanian Consulate in Edinburgh to act as interpreter.

Finally, the girls could tell their story from the day of their capture to landing on a cold Scottish beach in the middle of the night. Of a long wait in a bitterly cold tunnel and angry men talking in a language they didn't understand. Of a long journey in the back of a van and a lengthy stop during which they heard more angry exchanges. Of another long journey until, at last, the door of the van opened onto a hillside as dark was falling again. Of being forced out and left alone as the last of the light faded. Of stumbling around hoping and failing to see any signs of life until the danger of walking on rough ground in the pitch dark forced them to huddle for shelter in the lee of some rocks. Of losing hope then being found by Max.

However difficult their past and uncertain their future, they were finally safe among people who would look after them. Mary would make sure of that.

Driving over the bleak summit of Soutra on the final leg of their journey from Manchester Airport to Edinburgh, Anya Arbuthnot and Kadir Demercol were surprised to see a small convoy of police cars, paramedic vehicles and a car with diplomatic plates coming towards them before turning off onto a hillside track ahead.

"You would wonder what sort of major, international incident would necessitate a turn-out like that in a remote area like this," Kadir remarked.

"More than a few hillwalkers in trouble for sure," Anya replied. They had no idea that they had just driven past a crucial link to the death of Hafez Yilmaz.

Chapter 15
Fugitives April 1997

Glasgow Airport was crowded—an unbroken mass of tightly packed, winding queues moving at snail's pace towards check-in desks. Trolleys piled with luggage and small children impeded movement while harassed staff struggled through the chaos in search of final passengers for imminently departing flights. An unbroken stream of barely intelligible announcements issued passenger advice that fell on deafened ears. Adding to the confusion, intermittent bursts of sun-drenched, beach-clad arrivals clutching toy donkeys, sombreros and screaming children battled their way through the confusion towards the exits.

Yasmin realised that trying to make a run for it through the tightly packed, corralled lines of stressed travellers was not going to work. Orhan held her arm in a steel-like grip as they stood in line at the check-in desk. Immediately behind her, Orhan's henchmen, whom she only knew as Jazz and Greg, were seriously invading what little personal space airport conditions allowed. At the sight of Ulrich pushing his way through the queue to join them after getting rid of the car, her heart sank further.

"Don't make a fuss!" Orhan hissed as they were called forward to the check-in desk, his grip loosening momentarily as he leant forward to hand over their passports and tickets. Yasmin managed to pull herself free but was immediately checked by Ulrich who had moved forward, ostensibly to help load their luggage onto the belt. The woman at check-in asked Ulrich to step back behind the line, but it was too late for Yasmin. Orhan had regained his grip on her arm.

"I don't want to go on this flight!" Yasmin announced, trying desperately to catch the woman's attention as she was being dragged away.

"She's afraid of flying," Orhan intervened, flashing a benevolent, conspiratorial smile towards everyone within earshot.

Completely misunderstanding the little scene playing out before her and anxious to process the remaining passengers, the check-in assistant attempted to reassure Yasmin, "You'll be alright once you are on the aircraft—I have given you an aisle seat, just don't look out of the window. Lots of people are scared the first time they fly."

At security, Yasmin deliberately left her belt on under her sweater hoping that the buckle would set off the scanner alarm and she would be taken aside for a body check. It did trigger the alarm and she was stopped by security staff, but she was not taken aside. Passengers were milling all around her; Orhan had noticed what was happening and had moved towards her, the check was perfunctory, and her belt was removed and passed through the scanner. Security staff turned away immediately after telling her she could go and collect her belongings from the luggage belt.

"I am being forced onto this flight," she called out. Security staff passed a quizzical glance in her direction, shrugged their shoulders, and moved on to deal with the impatient queue forming up to be body-checked.

"One more trick like that and you'll be handed over to Jazz and Greg who have all sorts of ways of ensuring your silence," Orhan threatened as he marched her swiftly through the departures lounge towards their gate.

"I need to go to the loo."

"Wait until you are on the plane."

"I can't wait—I'll shit myself!"

Exasperated, Orhan marched her to the ladies' toilet accompanied by Jazz and Greg who took up positions immediately outside. Orhan went to a small bar near the gate to order coffee. Yasmin decided to stay in the toilet until the Bodrum flight left; however, after fifteen minutes, Orhan convinced a passing cleaner that he was worried about his sister, explaining that she was terrified of flying and was probably 'in a bit of a state.' The woman obligingly went into the toilet and found Yasmin who refused to leave, saying she was being forced onto the flight by her brother. Assuming this was no more than flight phobia, the woman told her that she couldn't stay in the toilet area and that if she didn't leave, she would have to call security.

For a moment, Yasmin thought this might save her. She would have time to explain to security staff what was happening without being overheard by Orhan. Then she realised that Orhan would be waiting outside on his own, exuding charm and concern, convincing staff that his beloved sister was simply having a panic attack and that he would look after her. Reluctantly, she left and as predicted, Orhan took hold of her as soon as she stepped outside, flashing an insincere smile and genuine words of thanks to the cleaner. He pushed Yasmin roughly onto a seat between Ulrich and Jazz and handed her a coffee.

"Drink that and pull yourself together."

The coffee was lukewarm and had a slightly metallic taste. *Cheap coffee grounds* she thought to herself, but she was thirsty and drank it. Waves of tiredness flooded over her and the voices around her sounded remote. She felt strangely weak, and it was an effort to get up and move forward for boarding. She woke up three hours into the flight, struggling to make sense of where she was, how she had got there or where she was going. She was in the middle seat towards the rear of the plane, Jazz next to her in the window seat and Orhan in the aisle seat. A memory of the woman at the check-in desk emerged through her confusion—didn't she say that I had an aisle seat? Odd. Why am I in the middle seat? Slowly, as her mind cleared, confusion gave way to outrage.

"Why are you doing this to me?" She asked in a deliberately loud voice causing passengers across the aisle to look on in mild disapproval, fearing a domestic altercation was about to break out.

"Stop making a scene!" Orhan hissed gripping her arm so tightly it hurt. "It's because you know too much—you and your spying Turkish boyfriend. Do you realise your meddling has wrecked an important business deal leaving me in debt to people I'd rather not owe money to!"

"Orhan, I have no idea what you are talking about, or what Hafez has to do with anything."

"I suppose you thought he kept appearing at the restaurant because he liked you, you stupid idiot. He was spying! Spying on me and poking his nose into my business."

"Don't be ridiculous, Orhan. None of us knows anything about your business, nor do we want to know. What exactly do you think a spy might have picked up from your rare appearances at the restaurant with your nasty chums? — That you bully your family, eat vast quantities of food, frighten customers, and leave without paying? Why would knowing what a horrible person you are, endanger your so-called business?" Yasmin realised that she had raised her voice again attracting even more attention from fellow passengers.

"Keep your voice down, you silly bitch! It was you who asked Yilmaz to come to your party. Why else would a solitary guy who doesn't drink or chat up women come to a party at a nightclub if not to spy on me? Did you know he left the party that night to follow me?"

Yasmin froze. "And…?"

"You ask too many questions."

"What has happened to Hafez?"

"Nothing that concerns you!"

Yasmin's response was cut short by the arrival of unwanted food, and she could only watch in disgust as Orhan and Jazz demolished theirs and hers.

"I asked about Hafez."

"And I told you to shut up."

"You have no right to treat me like this—this is a kidnap and as soon as I can, I am going to report you to the police. And if you have hurt Hafez, so much worse for you. You are no longer my brother!"

"I have every right to treat you however I want when you have ruined my business. And I have no need of a sister who has betrayed her family. This is a matter of honour now."

The mention of honour terrified her. Ice-cold fear gripped her mind. She knew what so-called 'honour' meant to thugs like her brother. Could Orhan actually go as far as to kill her? A sideways glance at his flushed, angry face told her the answer. There was no point in making the situation worse by arguing further. Her focus now had to be on escape. Her priority would be to retrieve her passport at Bodrum airport. She still had her phone though no charger but there should be enough battery power left to call her father and get him to wire money through to the nearest branch of Western Union.

As the flight prepared for landing, she ventured to ask, "So what happens now?"

"We will be staying in holiday accommodation owned by distant relatives of mine in Bodrum."

"Distant relatives of mine too, presumably! Who are they? I have never heard of relatives living in Bodrum."

"I told you to hold your tongue."

"I want my passport back."

"Not now."

"That's theft." Orhan gave a short laugh. There was no answer to her demand and no passport either.

Chapter 16
Arrival in Bodrum, Türkiye

There were no opportunities to escape at immigration. Her one attempt to retrieve her passport at the visa desk came to nothing. As she leant forward to collect it from the immigration official, Orhan yanked her arm back so hard it almost dislocated her shoulder. The official looked on disapprovingly but said nothing. Yasmin was in tears.

In the arrivals hall, they were met by a heavily built, middle-aged man. There was not a flicker of welcome in his dark, sullen eyes. He told them to follow him without a word of introduction. At the car park, they were ushered into a beaten-up 4×4 and driven along the coast for about eight kilometres in utter silence. Leaving the coast and smart tourist areas behind, he turned inland and after another bone-shaking kilometre pulled up at a run-down concrete house. It was single-storey, the ground around it strewn with rubbish.

"So much for holiday accommodation!" was Yasmin's first thought. The man—presumably their 'distant relative,' opened the house, threw the keys onto a worn kitchen table and told them to keep out of sight until told otherwise. His wife would bring some food later.

The food, when it arrived, was inedible—a bowl of evil-smelling bean stew and some stale bread. The wife of the 'distant relative'—presumably also a distant relative—was a taciturn woman. Her small, dark eyes glared out from under a badly arranged headscarf and her round body was shrouded in a dirty brown chador. She remained silent as she arranged the table and did not respond to Orhan's questions. "Husband come later," was all she said as the door closed behind her.

No one felt like eating. The smell of the food mingled with the smell of anxious, unwashed men turned Yasmin's stomach. The heat was intense inside what was little more than a concrete box with windows firmly shuttered against prying eyes. Tempers frayed and arguments broke out about what to do next—not that they had much choice in the matter. Orhan's attempts to reassure the group that his 'relatives' would find safe houses for them increasingly fell on deaf ears. Yasmin's hopes of retrieving her passport while Orhan slept had long since faded. Throughout that long, hot day, his eyes rarely closed, opening with a start at the least noise, while his accomplices took turns to stand guard. Even if she did manage to escape, she knew that without a passport, visa, or money, she had no way of getting back to the airport. Nothing in her previous, well-ordered life had prepared her for this. All she could do was wait and watch for an opportunity to save herself.

The 'relative' duly appeared late that evening. "You can't stay here. I need you gone by tonight," was all he said. No explanation was forthcoming for the change of plan, provoking an uproar of angry voices. "Why? What's happened? You said we could stay here until things got sorted out!"

"The police are looking for you. Called at our house today—seem very anxious to trace the girl. We want nothing to do with whatever you are involved in, Orhan. A van will call for you just after midnight. Be ready!"

"To take us where?"

"Istanbul."

"Istanbul!"

"Easier to hide in a city than in a small village like this. Better for you, better for us."

"What will we do in Istanbul?"

"That's for you to work out—we'll take you somewhere safe. That's all I can do. I can't risk having you here any longer."

A storm of protest broke out as the man left, locking the door behind him.

"So much for living in a quiet coastal resort until the heat died down!"

"It's barely twenty-four hours since we arrived and already the police are on our trail! How did that happen?"

"I don't trust that 'relative' of yours, Orhan—what did you say his name was? Don't trust him at all. What on earth are we going to do in Istanbul, assuming we ever get there?"

"Of course, he won't take us to Istanbul—it's at least a 10-hour journey from here. This is just a ruse to get rid of us in some quiet spot on the way."

Orhan glared at the assembled group; anger, fear and frustration building up to towering rage. Yasmin had seen the signs before and backed slowly into a dark corner.

The noise of a van pulling up at midnight frayed everyone's nerves to breaking point. As heavy footsteps approached across the rough ground outside, they instinctively moved away from the door. The sight of the thick-set hooded man who opened the door did nothing to allay fears, nor did the all-too-visible bulge of a gun in the waistband of a second man following closely behind. Although the unwelcome intruders' hoods and heavy beards made recognition all but impossible, Orhan was sure he had never met either before. There was no sign of his 'relative' and this alarmed Orhan.

"Sen kimsin?" (Who are you?)

"Seni ilgilenditmez. (Not your concern) Eşyalarini topla ve minibüse bin! (Collect your stuff and get into the van!)"

The second man shoved them none too gently out of the house, down the path and into the back of the van. There were no seats, just a few filthy cushions scattered across some equally filthy rugs.

"You can't expect us to travel all the way to Istanbul in this!" Orhan hissed at the driver—in panic forgetting that he didn't understand English. The sight of a gun pulled in response was all that was needed to make the group acquiesce. As the van doors were shut and locked, the overpowering smell of diesel fumes mixed with other unpleasant odours intensified making Yasmin want to vomit. Just before dawn, the van turned off a main road and pulled over after a few hundred metres. The back doors opened and they were ordered out one at a time at gunpoint; each sure that this was to be their place of execution—only to realise that it was nothing more fatal than an open-air toilet stop. Relieved in more senses than one, they got back into the van rubbing painful limbs as they sat down. No food or water was offered, but being alive was good enough for the moment.

By mid-morning on this seemingly endless journey, every part of their bodies ached, and only extreme discomfort kept fitful sleep at bay. They could hear traffic intensify and before long, they recognised the slow stop-start of urban driving. Muffled sounds could occasionally be heard over the grinding of the ancient diesel engine, street vendors plying their wares, the shouts of children and a distant call to prayer all stark reminders that normal life continued beyond their present precarious existence.

The van gradually began to pick up speed again and Yasmin's faint hopes receded. The sounds of normal life had been vaguely reassuring and she felt fear mounting again in the absence of any sound bar the noise of the engine. A sharp turn to the right threw them all in a tangle of limbs towards one side of the van. They were no longer being driven on a smooth road and continued to be thrown around as the van negotiated potholes, sharp corners and rough terrain. All of a sudden, the driver braked hard and the van came to a juddering stop. The back door opened and they were ushered out at gunpoint, amid imprecations at their slowness as they tried to restore circulation to stiffened limbs.

Yasmin looked around in despair at the vast industrial wasteland which stretched as far as the eye could see on three sides. In the far distance, she could make out a line of low, rolling hills. No sign of human life broke the landscape of abandoned buildings. A rambling plant she didn't recognise spread its tentacles along crumbling walls and coarse grasses broke through the rubble on what had once been access roads. Roofs had caved in on many of the buildings and jagged spars of broken traves reached up to an empty sky. Large metal doors had once secured the building in front of them, and it was towards these doors that she and the others were led. High up on the cement wall, a series of barred windows stared sightlessly on the unexpected intruders, shards of their long-lost glass littering the ground below. Were they all going to be shot and left to rot in this nameless wilderness?

Surely, they would not have been driven all the way to Istanbul—if this was indeed Istanbul—to be murdered. That could have been done with much less effort nearer to Bodrum. Wherever this was, it bore no resemblance to the photographs of Istanbul which lined the walls of her parents' restaurant. Where was the magnificent dome of Hagia Sofia, or the minarets of the Blue Mosque? Where were the fabulous gardens of Top Kapi or the Galata Bridge linking Europe to Asia, or Dolmabaçe Palace and the Bosphorus shimmering in the sunshine? Wherever this was, it was not the Istanbul of her dreams.

As if in answer to her fears, they were hustled into one of the more intact buildings. Three men looked up from a game of cards being played on an upturned barrel. Hard faces and even harder eyes turned in their direction. The men were middle-aged, and everything from their grizzled hair and heavy beards to their loose-fitting trousers and long-sleeved, collarless shirts needed a good wash. There was a rapid exchange with the driver and money changed hands.

"You work for us now," the lead card player said. "No work, no food..." he added, his harsh laugh displaying a keyboard of blackened teeth. "Men work, not the girl!" the unpleasant smile transformed into a leer as he spoke.

"The girl is my sister. Don't you dare touch her!" Yasmin turned in astonishment at this uncharacteristically protective gesture from Orhan. Bravado exhausted by this outburst,

Orhan did nothing more than stare sullenly as their captor continued, "Sister stay here—make sure you come back at night."

Life as captives in a wasteland slowly assumed a rhythm. Yasmin was kept in the building to make what she could of the sporadic deliveries of food. No one was in any doubt that she was being held hostage to ensure that Orhan and his accomplices did as they were told. Her attempts to strike up some sort of relationship with her captors were rebuffed—the only relationship that might have interested them on fragile hold following Orhan's outburst. Orhan, Jazz, Ulrich and Greg were taken out daily to sell drugs on streets where well-off Istanbülus and tourists would fear to tread unless they had a very compelling habit.

Yasmin did her best to keep track of time. According to her calculations, they had been held in the building for twenty-two days, meaning it was now the end of April. Unlike the others, she still had her phone though it had long since run out of charge. All other phones had been taken by their captors along with their passports and money, leaving the men with just the burner phones provided for their new line of business. One of their captors had searched her clothing and bag looking for a phone but had found nothing. On the journey from Bodrum, she remembered the story of a kidnap victim who had concealed her phone inside a sanitary pad packed in her wash bag. Fumbling around in the darkened van, she had managed to extract a single pad and nail scissors. Making a small slit in the covering, she slid her phone in between the absorbent layers and replaced the pad in the middle of the pack. And there it remained.

A row broke out among the men that night. It began with an argument about money, or rather the lack of it reaching the pockets of Orhan and his friends. It exploded into violence when their captors said they were being paid in kind by being kept safe and provided with accommodation and food.

"Call this food," Orhan yelled tipping over the plank which served as a table, sending watery humous, stale bread and desiccated falafel to the filthy floor. As this was all the food on offer, the others were not a hundred per cent behind this act of defiance. Yasmin managed to restore calm by pointing out that they could probably be heard miles away and Orhan and his entourage retreated into an angry huddle at the far end of the room.

"I think I am being followed," Greg told them anxiously. He was tall, a scattering of freckles covered all exposed skin and with his red hair and beard he was the least likely to be able to blend in with the crowds. "I can't speak Turkish and if the police stop me with drugs and false ID, I'll be for the high jump."

"What makes you think you are being followed by the police?"

"He's dressed in civvies, but something about the way he moves makes me think he's a cop."

"You sure he's following you?"

"Saw him yesterday and today. He is good. When I tried to give him the slip by hiding behind bins in an alleyway, he ran past me and stood at the end of the alley looking in both directions. I went back the way I came and saw a police car cruising around. I'm scared."

"Should we tell our charming hosts?"

Before anyone could answer, one of the charming hosts came over and in a menacing whisper, told them to shut up. As the sound of approaching vehicles grew louder, their captors doused the oil lamps, motioning for complete silence while their leader climbed up into the roof space to look through a gap. They heard his muttered imprecation, "Shit—the police!"

To Yasmin's horror, Orhan, Jazz, Ulrich and Greg were surrounded at gunpoint and pushed out of the door towards the captors' van. She retreated soundlessly into the furthest corner of the room, shaking in fear as she listened intently to the sounds from outside. She heard shouted commands in Turkish, followed by shots being fired. The shooting seemed to last an eternity although it was probably all over in a few minutes. A vehicle started up—was it the captors' van or a police car? She couldn't be sure. More shots were fired as the vehicle pulled away; then an eerie silence fell. More voices this time, shouting orders down phones and she was sure she picked up the word 'ambulans'—ambulance. Nervously, she climbed into the roof space, checking each step before shifting her weight in the near-total darkness. No sooner had she reached the gap in the roof, than she heard the door burst open and the glare of light in the floor below almost blinded her.

"Police! Drop your weapons! Raise your arms!"

Yasmin's arms were half up before she realised that the police couldn't see her. Heads down and continuing to shout, they were making their way meticulously through the various sections of the building. One man knelt to study the spilt food while others raked through scattered belongings.

"All clear!"

The building was plunged into darkness once more and she heard sirens approaching—two different sirens, presumably more police cars and ambulances. She plucked up the courage to peer through the gap in the roof and the sight that met her eyes froze her to the bone. Five men lay on the ground, one moving spasmodically; the others still. One of the silent bodies wore a police uniform. She couldn't identify anyone else until a policeman kicked over one of the bodies and shone a torch on his face revealing blood-stained red hair. Greg. Whether Orhan had escaped or was lying on the ground, she couldn't tell—and realised she no longer cared.

The fact that a policeman had been killed in the shoot-out, answered the question she had been asking herself, "Should she give herself up to the police and hope to be able to explain her situation?" With one of their own men dead, the police would be in no mood to ask questions, let alone listen to explanations. The drug dealers' van had disappeared and a helicopter with a powerful searchlight was circling the area. Police and ambulance staff were still dealing with the bodies, but she knew it wouldn't be long before they turned their attention to a detailed search of the building. They would find her bag and sooner or later, they would find her phone. She had to retrieve them. As quickly as she dared, she climbed back down from the roof, grabbed her bag, and had just reached the sanctuary of the roof space again as the door opened to allow white-clad forensics experts to enter and set up field lights.

Yasmin realised she would be spotted if she stayed in the roof space. The lighting below let her see another gap in the roof towards the back of the building. It looked just about large enough for her to squeeze through once the coast was clear. Reaching it was another matter. She would need to crawl along the rafters in a half crouch position knowing that any moment she might lose her balance, or a rafter might give way sending her plunging to her death below. Reluctantly, she decided she would have to leave her bag behind—it would take every ounce of nerve and all the balancing skill she possessed to make her way safely along the rafters without adding the destabilising weight of a bag on her back. As there was no longer any need to hide her phone, she extracted it from its hiding place and slid it into the back pocket of her jeans.

She had no idea whether her passport was still in the building or whether it had been taken by their captors. Either way, she was unlikely to see it again. If the police found her passport, she could only hope that they would conclude that it had been stolen. The more likely conclusion that the owner of the passport had been party to drug dealing, illegal use of firearms and the murder of a police officer terrified her. Forcing herself to focus on the immediate danger of discovery, she began the slow, heart-stopping crawl along a rafter. Each time it creaked under her weight, she was sure her last moment had come. Either the rafter would give way, or the noise would alert the forensic team below.

"What was that?" She heard one of them ask after a particularly loud creak. She sensed the stillness of the people below as they listened intently for further sounds.

"Probably just rats—these buildings must be full of them," someone concluded.

After what seemed like an age, she reached the gap at the back of the building and cautiously pulled herself out onto a solid section of the rooftop. Upright, she could see over the apex onto the tops of the vehicles below. If she could see, she could be seen, not least if the helicopter returned. For the moment, she was just thankful that the sound of its rotors had faded into the distance. She flattened herself onto the roof and prepared for a long, cold wait until the last of the police vehicles left. The wait gave her time to take stock of her desperate situation. She did not know where she was, she knew no one in Türkiye, she had no ID—though she was far from sure that she wanted to be identified in the circumstances—and she had no money. She had no food and more importantly, no water. She hadn't showered or changed her outer clothes in almost a month. The only positives she could come up with were that she was alive, looked Turkish and spoke the language fluently.

As dawn broke, she saw the last of the ambulances and police cars leave. Her newest problem was how to get down from the roof. She had heard the doors being locked and padlocked after the forensics team left and knew all too well there was no other way out of the building. From her position halfway up the sloping roof, she would have to make her way across a stretch of broken tiles to the edge and hope for some footholds on the descent to the ground. The prospect of multiple fractures could spell the end for her.

Who would find her in this wilderness if she couldn't walk out on her own two feet? Lying flat and coaxing frozen limbs back into service, Yasmin stretched one leg downwards until her foot got a grip on a secure joint. Her next move was fraught with danger as she shifted her weight to allow her other foot to find a grip. It didn't, sending a stream of tiles crashing down to the ground below. Her leg flailed around before finally finding a grip and Yasmin froze, unable to move forwards or backwards, worried that the police might have left someone behind to guard the property. If they had, that person would know this was not a noise made by rats. No one came to investigate and after a few minutes, her heart rate steadied sufficiently to allow her to continue her precarious descent.

Finally, her feet touched the guttering at the edge of the roof, and she tested it for strength. It seemed to hold. She let her legs drop over the edge, but her feet found no hold below and as her weight transferred, she lost control of her descent, grabbing frantically at the guttering to arrest her fall. An agonising second later, the guttering gave way, and she was in free fall. The advice of her old PE teacher flashed into her mind, 'If you fall from a height, bend your knees, curl into a ball and roll as you land.' (Later, she would look back in wonder at her brain's ability to retrieve vital, long-forgotten information in moments of crisis.)

Seconds later, she lay in a crumpled heap trying to assess the level of damage, waiting for the pain to kick in. She didn't have to wait for long. She had rolled to the right, and her right shoulder and hip were extremely painful. Her right arm was numb, and blood ran down the right side of her face from a cut somewhere on her forehead. She tried to move each of her limbs in turn and miraculously, they all seemed to be working albeit painfully. She tried to get up, clutching the wall for support, her head spinning. She was alive and nothing was broken. So far, so good but the cuts and grazes on her face and arms needed to be cleaned and she had no access to water or antiseptic. As far as she could tell, her phone had survived the fall. The screen was intact, but until she had a chance to charge the device, there was no way of knowing if it was still working.

For the first time since she was a child, she broke down in tears, sobs wracking her chest intensifying the pain of her bruised, possibly cracked ribs.

'Pull yourself together and think!' Unfortunately, her PE teacher had left no additional advice to cover her present circumstances. She would walk into the city seeking help—but from whom? Was there a British Embassy in Istanbul? No, that would be in Ankara. Maybe there would be a Consulate—she could ask someone. First of all, she had to get out of this wasteland before any surviving gang members returned to look for her and before the police returned. Which way to go? Her instinct told her the city centre would be westwards, away from the hills.

After an agonising half hour of twists and turns over broken ground, Yasmin found what might have been the main access road into the industrial estate. It was in no better shape than the roads she had already walked over, but at least it was broad and straight promising that it might lead back to civilisation. Finding water was her most pressing problem. She had looked inside several of the buildings hoping to find a working tap, but without success. She was very thirsty but what worried her most was the sensation of heat in one of the cuts on her arm. The first sign of infection. She needed to find clean water quickly, but where and how? Did Istanbul have public water fountains like many cities in hot countries?

She supposed it would, but probably not on the outskirts, and people would look askance at a filthy woman trying to use a drinking water fountain to clean bleeding limbs. The same would be even truer in the courtyards of mosques where there was always water. Besides, her top was sleeveless and she had no headscarf, all of which ruled out the possibility of finding help at a mosque.

Chapter 17
Tayside Police
Headquarters Dundee

George McAllister and John joined DI Taylor in his office to mull over what they had learned at the *Izmir* and how any of it fitted with what else they knew about Hafez's final hours. The coffee was every bit as bad as the stuff they served in Lothian and Borders police stations, but it was warm and wet and helped them concentrate. It now seemed certain that Hafez had been at Yasmin's party at the *Marmaris*; that he had disappeared that night, most likely travelling to Cove where his motor bike was found, his body washed ashore further along the coast three days later.

The pathologist's provisional estimate was that he had been dead for at least 48 hours before his body was found and that he had not died by drowning. He had been tortured prior to death suggesting that he knew something or was thought to know something, and his captors had wanted to know with whom, if anyone, he might have shared this information. Orhan's sudden flight to Türkiye taking his sister and close associates with him hinted strongly at a link with Hafez's murder.

McAllister's phone rang and he moved away from the table to take the call.

"DC Singh, Sir. Thought you'd want to know—the manager at the Sheraton remembers a well-dressed man fitting Hafez's description reading in the hotel lounge for about two hours early Saturday evening. He didn't meet anyone and did not attend a function. He ordered tea and biscuits, paid by card at 20.05 and left."

"Can you ask the manager for the card receipt?"

"I have it, Sir, and the last four digits of the card number match Hafez's card. The debit also shows on his bank statement."

"Good work, Detective Constable."

"Thank you, Sir."

McAllister was about to close the call when DC Singh seemed to have an afterthought, "Curious case has just come in, Sir. Some young foreign girls were found wandering near Soutra early this morning. They were taken in by a farmer and his wife. Police and social workers are with them along with an interpreter from the Romanian Consulate. Just wondered if this might be linked to the case you are working on. Sorry if this is just wasting your time, Sir."

"Far from it, Detective Constable. Thank you—it may well be linked to our murder case. In the meantime, I want you to find out all you can about the *Marmaris*—who owns it, who runs it on a day-to-day basis, was there a register or guest list for that party, is there a record of any previous trouble at the club. I'll be back at the station tomorrow and we can discuss how to proceed depending on what you have found out."

A young man showing promise, he thought as he returned to the table to pass on all he had heard. They now knew where Hafez had spent the early part of the evening and could calculate roughly what time he would have arrived at the party. Questions abounded but answers remained stubbornly in the realms of hypothesis. Knowing Hafez's history, had he been following a lead? Had Orhan added trafficking young girls to his already grim CV? Was this what Hafez had found out and what ultimately cost him his life? And did these young Romanian girls fit into the picture somehow? If they had been trafficked, how and why had they ended up on a remote hillside miles away from the coast? Had Hafez's intervention threatened to expose a deal? Did someone decide the girls were damaged goods? If so, why release them rather than silence them? McAllister chipped in at this point,

"Orhan Cilic is many things, none of them good but I think even he would baulk at murdering children. We need to contact the Organised Crime Unit to find out who among gangland's finest might be interested in buying underage girls. If we know that, we may be able to trace a deal-gone-wrong back to Cilic."

Kadir and Anya were waiting for John at an old haunt of his, *Mother India* in Infirmary Street. While a stream of delicately spiced dishes arrived at their table, John brought them up-to-date with the investigation.

"We saw the commotion at Soutra!" Anya and Kadir chorused in unison. "We wondered what on earth could have brought a motorcade of police and emergency vehicles to an isolated hillside."

At that moment, Kadir's phone rang and he went outside to take the call. Fifteen minutes later, he returned, breathless with excitement.

"Cilic and friends did contact his so-called relative in Bodrum but moved on the same day. My colleagues have questioned the family in Bodrum who say they left of their own volition, and they have no idea where they have gone. We have detained the father and son for further questioning as we are unconvinced by their claim not to know by what means their visiting relatives left Bodrum, where they were heading, or what prompted their precipitate departure."

Kadir decided to return to Istanbul immediately to follow developments. At some point, Orhan and his entourage would need to draw money and use their cards or phones and Kadir wanted to be there as soon as they were traced. He had serious questions to ask about the death of Hafez and the abduction of Yasmin. John would travel with him, but first, he had to report back to DI McAllister and his DCI. It was clear that the trafficking of minors and Hafez Yilmaz's death were linked, and the link was Orhan Cilic. Leaving Kadir at his hotel in Edinburgh, John headed for police headquarters where he was met by George McAllister and taken to a room where a sullen DCI informed them that the superintendent would join the meeting.

After hearing John's report, the superintendent made it clear that George McAllister had to focus his resources on the trafficking of minors into Scotland and the suspected involvement of the Mansons. He accepted the argument that Lothian and Borders police had a strong interest in the death of Hafez Yilmaz, and the abduction of Yasmin Cilic, but was content to leave the Turkish police to lead on both cases for the time being, rejecting John's suggestion that George McAllister should go to Türkiye to liaise with police forces there. At the end of the meeting, it was agreed that as John was already going on a planned holiday to Türkiye with his wife, he could represent the interests of the Scottish police forces involved in both cases. George was relieved—he had never ventured further than the Channel Islands and the idea of being alone in Istanbul terrified him.

The superintendent was pleased that a way forward had been found which would satisfy public interest without placing additional demands on tight budgets. By contrast, the DCI had reverted to her default state of furious. The further involvement of John Arbuthnot, whom she preferred to view as a loose cannon rather than admit to professional jealousy, was intolerable. As he left the room, the superintendent turned around, "Just remember you are doing this in an unofficial capacity, John—but anything you find that might help tie up loose ends here would be much appreciated. I am afraid we can't offer any help with expenses though."

Some things never changed.

It would be several weeks before an unconnected drugs raid at a derelict warehouse on the outskirts of Istanbul revealed Orhan's destination.

Chapter 18
Cairo

Finding flights to Istanbul for the following morning proved difficult. A major international conference on the treatment of trauma was taking place at Istanbul University and flights were fully booked. Finally, a harassed travel agent managed to find a far-from-ideal solution: early morning flights from Edinburgh to London—London to Cairo; and an evening connection from Cairo to Istanbul. Kadir was doing his best to conceal his frustration at the delay when John asked,

"Do you know if Hafez's former colleague Daniele Antar still lives in Alexandria? If he remained in touch with Hafez, he might know something about what he was up to. We have a five-and-a-half-hour layover in Cairo; perhaps we could meet him somewhere."

"It's a long shot, but I'll see if I can get hold of him. I think I still have his number in my phone."

Kadir went outside to make the call and came back 15 minutes later. "That was a difficult call to make. Daniele didn't know that Hafez had died, and the news obviously upset him. He said he had received two voice mail messages yesterday from Hafez's father, both asking him to call back, but he had been so busy tying up loose ends at the hospital that he hadn't got around to doing so. He is going to the conference at Istanbul University and will be on the same flight as us. However, he suggests meeting for an early supper in Cairo as it will be easier to talk without being overheard in a restaurant than at the airport."

The restaurant Daniele had chosen overlooked the historic Hanging Church dedicated to the Virgin Mary and one of the oldest Coptic churches in Egypt.

"How did it get its name?" John asked, fearing some historic inter-religious atrocity.

Daniele laughed, "If you look closely, you will see that the nave overhangs a passageway underneath—nothing more sinister than that."

For a moment, tension lightened but as soon as a waiter left with their order, it gripped the three of them again. Daniele looked fit but decidedly more care-worn than the last time Kadir saw him in Siracusa. Lines had appeared on his deeply tanned face and silver threads ran through his dark hair.

"Have you heard from Hafez recently?" Kadir asked.

"To be honest, we had only just begun to exchange messages again. When I was forced to leave the clinic in Sicily, I was so angry with Hafez that I never wanted to see him again…And now I won't…" After a brief pause, he continued, "To begin with, I couldn't settle in Alexandria, or anywhere for that matter—so I joined Red Crescent medics working in Lebanon for six months. After that, I returned to Alexandria and am working in the trauma unit at the main hospital. I still spend one month a year with the Red Crescent though."

"That doesn't surprise me," Kadir said. "You and Hafez worked for Médecins Sans Frontières for several years, after all."

Daniele smiled wistfully, "These were good years—until the end—until civil unrest erupted into full-scale civil war and Amara was murdered. Hafez has been on a crusade ever since. Or at least he was. He contacted me, out of the blue, about ten months ago to say he was working as a researcher in Scotland and that people were being very kind, but he was finding it hard to settle. After that, we exchanged messages occasionally and not long ago, I suggested coming to Scotland to see him. When he didn't reply, I assumed he wasn't ready to see me again and left it at that."

"I don't suppose he said anything to you about a trip to Edinburgh, or about following a lead on people traffickers."

"Oh, not again! — Is that what got him killed? If that was what he was doing, I would be the last person he would confide in—not after all that happened in Siracusa."

"Any idea whom he might have confided in?"

"None at all. He mentioned being friendly with a girl he had met at a Turkish restaurant, and with one of his colleagues—a man I think—but I didn't get the impression that either was a particularly close relationship."

They had drawn a blank, but it had been a very pleasant way to pass the time before their late evening flight.

*

In Istanbul, time dragged on without finding any trace of Orhan and his accomplices. The 'relatives' in Bodrum finally admitted that they had insisted on the group leaving but stated under oath that they did not know the identity of the van driver or where he had dropped them off. They thought they might have overheard Orhan mention Istanbul to the driver but couldn't be sure. They professed ignorance as to who had arranged the transport, saying that Orhan must have contacted someone he knew. Kadir was convinced that they were lying, but whether they were interviewed separately or together, they stuck to their carefully rehearsed story; carefully rehearsed with the rather seedy lawyer who accompanied them, no doubt. Exhaustive searches of ports, airports, hotels and boarding houses in Istanbul had drawn a complete blank.

In an uncharacteristic show of temper, Kadir slapped his hands down on his desk, making John jump.

"Three weeks! Three weeks and not a trace of them! It's as if they have vanished into thin air. And thin air must be what they are living on. As far as we can work out, all the money they had with them would be the £100 Orhan drew out at Edinburgh Airport, and perhaps the £300 in Spanish pesetas that Yasmin had bought for her cancelled holiday to Majorca. We have checked the bank accounts of the relatives in Bodrum and there have been no significant cash withdrawals from there. None of the group's cards has been used and their phones are no longer active.

"They must be out of funds by now, not least because they will have had to resort to illegal money changers to get Turkish lire for their foreign currency. At best, they will have got about half the real value of their cash to cover expenses for five people for two weeks. This is an expensive city to be stranded in, so why have they not come to our attention by now for stealing or sleeping rough?"

John risked asking, "Do you think they might have made their way to Romania? Orhan presumably has contacts at that end of the trafficking chain—contacts who might be prepared to let him lie low for a while?"

"We have contacted the Romanian police. They apparently have an undercover officer working with traffickers in Bucharest, and he says that there have been no rumours of Orhan or his accomplices washing up in Bucharest or in Timisoara where the girls found in Scotland came from. He has confirmed, though, that the Mansons have got in on the act."

"How can they just have disappeared? It's beginning to look as if we will have to wait until one of them is arrested or turns up dead! It's Yasmin I worry about. The world Orhan operates in is no place for a decent young woman."

Kadir agreed.

With no leads to follow, John decided to return to Scotland.

"I will check on progress at the Scottish end with DI McAllister, although I am sure he would have let us know if there had been any significant developments in their investigation. I am also painfully aware that unless Orhan is found soon, our holiday plans will be in jeopardy, so we had better spend the next three weeks being model husbands to avoid being served with divorce papers if the trip has to be cancelled."

Kadir winced. This would not be the first family holiday that had had to be cancelled because of his work, and he knew how much Ayşe had been looking forward to exploring Türkiye with the Arbuthnots. He needed to find Orhan fast.

Chapter 19
Bearsden, Glasgow
May 1997

DI McAllister and DS Souter from Strathclyde Police were sitting in the lavishly furnished, taste-free lounge at the Manson's pretentious villa in Bearsden. Reg, the undisputed head of the family, had aged considerably since McAllister last saw him. He was confined to a wheelchair following a stroke, but his eyes had lost none of the steel and barely concealed outrage with which he was wont to challenge the police, or anyone else who caused him grief for that matter. And, not for the first time, his younger son Ronnie was causing him grief. Ronnie looked terrified and on the verge of tears. Rick, the older brother looked mutinous.

"As I have told you people many times over the years, I may not be a saint but the Mansons NEVER—I repeat NEVER—touch children." His sons joined in the obligatory chorus, but Ronnie looked pale, and beads of sweat stood out on his forehead.

Realising they were getting nowhere confronting the Mansons on their home turf, McAllister and Souter left, promising 'to keep in touch'.

Back in the car, McAllister turned to DS Souter, "We need to bring Ronnie in to interview him on his own. He is definitely hiding something but will never cough up if Reg is there to protect him. Can you set that up for us tomorrow please?"

"Delighted. I get the feeling that Ronnie would feel safer in an interview room at police headquarters than under interrogation at the Manson mansion."

"Meantime, I'll check with John in case there have been any developments at the Istanbul end."

The following morning, two uniformed officers called at the Manson villa to bring Ronnie in for questioning, only to be met by a household in mourning. Apparently, Ronnie's car had gone off the road at a dangerous curve on the B835 north of the village of Buchlyvie, overturned and burst into flames. By the time a passing motorist had reported the accident and emergency vehicles had arrived at the scene, the car was a charred wreck; its driver was unidentifiable. The only skid marks on the road were those of Ronnie's car; there was no evidence of any other vehicle being involved. The burnt-out carcass of the car was removed for forensic testing, but it was unlikely that any evidence of a fault or tampering would have survived the inferno.

Dental records would be required to identify the driver, but could there be any doubt about who that would prove to be? An elaborate cover-up to the detriment of some sacrificial acolyte could not be discounted. Reg Manson had been clear that the Mansons did not touch children—but did that exception extend to his son?

With the investigation stalled John returned briefly to Leigh-on-Sea to collect Anya and prepare for their holiday with the Demercols.

Chapter 20
Istanbul

Ushering his newly arrived guests onto a terrace overlooking the Bosphorus, Kadir seemed preoccupied rather than jubilant at the prospect of a well-earned holiday with good friends.

"Can I come too?" Anoushka, the Demercol's four-year-old 'surprise' child, lightened the mood as she always did. Her older siblings smiled indulgently. Rafa was 22 and studying for the bar and 20-year-old Sara was studying photography at a college of art.

"Not this time, darling; besides, it is time you were in bed."

"But I have had hardly any time with John and Anya and you are all leaving tomorrow. I'll be left with Rafa and Sara and they are so *boring!*"

"You would hate it, Anoushka. It will be a long car journey and we will be visiting a lot of ancient ruins and caves with nothing left inside them."

"Why are you going if there is nothing to see but a lot of old caves?"

"Time for bed, Madam. Maria will tell you a story if you are a good girl."

"Where did she come from?" Kadir asked as a disgruntled Anoushka stomped out of the room with her nanny.

"I rather hoped you might remember," Ayşe replied as a knowing smile passed between them—memories of a room overlooking Venice's Grand Canal, both convinced that menopause was firmly established. Wrongly convinced, as it transpired.

At that moment, no one would have been more surprised than Anoushka to know that twenty years later, she would be in the Australian outback looking for historic traces of indigenous people without the aid of ancient ruins to help with her research.

Lying in bed that night, Anya thought of John's daughter, Carole who had also had a late baby. Carole had followed her beloved stepfather into teaching and was married to a fellow teacher. They were happy, but money was tight.

"Childcare must be so much easier with household staff and a nanny," she mused, thinking of Carole juggling a career and the challenges involved in caring for two teenagers and a toddler.

*

A phone call came in as they were having breakfast the next morning. Kadir took the call and returned to the table fifteen minutes later. Clutching a cup of coffee, he took a deep breath.

"Do you want the good news or the bad news first?"

Ayşe and Anya shared resigned glances. Ayşe said, "You'd better give us the bad news first, Kadir."

"Twenty-four hours ago, the drugs squad carried out a raid at a warehouse in an abandoned industrial site. Unfortunately, there was a shoot-out during the raid and five men, including a police officer died at the scene. It seems that Cilic and his accomplices had been dealing for a Turkish gang. One of the Turkish gangsters is in custody being questioned. Cilic and two others escaped in a van. One of them is seriously injured. We believe Yasmin was held captive by the Turkish gang but may have managed to escape. That, at least, is the hope.

"The Bodrum police confirm that Orhan was accompanied by three men and one woman so we can assume she was with them at that point. The van was found this morning—it had run out of fuel about 15 kilometres to the south of Istanbul. Police are combing the area looking for the men as we speak. At least one of them will not be able to walk far. They did not find a woman in or around the warehouse, but they did find four UK passports in the jacket of one of the Turkish gang members; one of them Yasmin's. A fifth UK passport is unaccounted for. They also found a bag in the rafters with a few personal items belonging to a woman."

John interposed, barely concealing his interest, "If the police have found Orhan and his accomplices, I need to question them about Hafez; and if it is Orhan who is badly injured then the sooner the better. I would also like to keep an eye on the search for Yasmin—if she is found, I don't want some over-zealous police officer assuming she is part of a murderous drugs cartel and treating her accordingly."

Ayşe and Anya let out simultaneous groans.

Chapter 21
Escape from Captivity

By the time Yasmin reached the end of the access road where it intersected with a four-lane highway, she was beyond exhaustion. The mid-day sun beat down on the parched land and her eyes were smarting at the unaccustomed glare after weeks inside a dark warehouse. Raging thirst and a throbbing arm added to her distress and she sank down in the sparse shade of a crumbling wall to contemplate her precarious situation. On the far side of the highway, apartment blocks stretched as far as the eye could see but the thought of trying to cross over four lanes of fast-moving traffic robbed her of the last of her courage. Unbidden tears streaked through the fine dust on her face.

"Pull yourself together! My options: I can wait to die here, or I can play Russian roulette in the traffic—thanks to you, Orhan! OK. — I'll go for the second option. Now or never." Yasmin pulled herself painfully back onto her feet pausing for a few seconds till her head stopped spinning. Taking a deep breath, she launched herself into the fast-moving traffic dodging and swerving to a chorus of shouts, squealing brakes and blaring horns, accompanied by hand gestures that required no interpretation. To her surprise and immense relief, she arrived on the other side of the highway with no further damage to her already compromised body. She laughed hysterically at the lunacy of it all.

A series of narrow streets flanked by apartment blocks led away from the main road. Choosing one at random, she began to walk, thankful for the shade cast by the buildings. Most people passed by with barely a look in her direction, intent on their own concerns. Veiled women burdened with shopping bags and children headed homewards, and gaggles of school children poured out of a concrete and glass structure that looked as if it had seen better days. At one point, Yasmin had to step out into the road to avoid a group of sullen-looking men standing at a street corner. They stared at her, drawn by the sight of a strange woman in filthy, tattered western clothing—a different take on poverty and desperation from that pervading their neighbourhood.

Further on, she came to a small square with a market stall selling fruit and vegetables. While the stall-holder's attention was distracted by a customer, Yasmin lifted an apple. "So now I have become a thief! Well done, Orhan!" Diving into an alleyway, she sank her teeth into the apple letting the refreshing juice fill her parched mouth and drip down her chin. Nothing had ever tasted so wonderful. But it was water she really needed and stealing water wasn't so easy. Tantalising packs of bottled water stood at shop doorways, but making an undetected escape with one of these would be nigh impossible.

She trudged onwards, deepening shadows and a slight chill in the air telling her that the day was drawing to a close. After about two kilometres, the road she was on ended in a T junction. To her right, she saw an intersection with traffic lights and a signpost. Close up, the directions on the weathered signpost were difficult to make out, not least because she had never learned to read or write Turkish. She was about to give up the struggle when she noticed a small arrow above which she could identify s-hir m—k-zi. Sounding the letters over and over again she searched for a link with phonic Turkish, "sehir merkezi," she shouted in triumph, "city centre!" The road indicated did not look very promising, but as she had no idea where she was, following it seemed the best option. A steady stream of traffic filled the narrow street with dust and noise, pushing pedestrians onto crowded pavements.

Yasmin was almost delirious with thirst, and she found the crowd of bodies pushing past her this way and that was frightening. A young boy dodged past her, his backpack catching her injured arm and she almost fainted with pain. To make matters worse, she was increasingly aware of the intimidating looks she was attracting from passers-by. She had to escape from the crowds, and she absolutely had to find water.

Halfway down a side street, she took refuge under a rusty fire escape to wait until dusk when the rush hour might have abated. She lay her head against a rough brick wall and closed her eyes. A faint rhythmic sound coming from the far side of the wall lulled her to momentary sleep before waking her with a jolt. It was the sound of water dripping somewhere on the other side of the wall. Yasmin was on her feet in an instant looking for a way into the building.

An ancient arched doorway had been incorporated into a much later brick and cement structure. The stone arch still retained some of its original carvings, but the massive door which must once have hung there had gone. Through the arch, Yasmin could see a small courtyard occupied by an array of cars in various states of roadworthiness. A garage mechanics' workshop lay open on one side of the courtyard and an office occupied the side facing her. She worked out that the source of the drip must be near the wall opposite the workshop. Terrified of being seen, she crouched down low as she made her way between cars towards the wall. And there it was—a mirage; large drops of water dripping from a short hose attached to an external tap. Much as she wanted to, she didn't dare turn the tap full on in case it alerted someone to her presence. Instead, she let the drips fall into her parched mouth, long past caring about the source or purity of the water.

Thirst quenched, she cupped her hands and washed her face and arms as best she could. Cleansed of dirt, the wound on her arm looked red and angry. She left the courtyard as she had entered it, her heart in her mouth every time she heard a voice. What had happened to her? A few weeks ago, she would have had the confidence to ask for water and of course, a few weeks ago, she would have had the money to pay for it—not to mention money for decent clothes, a hotel room, and treatment for her arm.

Chapter 22
The Mosque Kitchen

Yasmin returned to her refuge under the fire escape until dusk fell and the smell of evening meals being prepared all but drove her crazy. Wearily, she got to her feet, aware that the sound of dripping water had ceased. Nonetheless, she crept around to the garage entrance again, hoping the courtyard would be deserted and she could turn the tap on. To her dismay, there were mechanics in the courtyard closing the service bays for the night. The tap had been turned off. No sooner had she decided to wait until everyone had left when a voice rang out, "Hey, you! What are you doing?"

Yasmin ran until she could run no further, collapsing onto a rickety chair abandoned outside a closed shop. She let herself cry—hard dry sobs where once there might have been wet tears. Through a haze of misery, she noticed a man moving towards her—a man in a police uniform. She mustn't get caught like this. Not in this filthy state. Not without a passport or identity card. Not on the day after a police officer had been shot by one of her brother's accomplices. Getting to her feet, she turned and walked away forcing herself to maintain a steady pace when every instinct told her to run. To her enormous relief, the policeman lost interest when she started to move.

Yasmin trudged on for hours in the general direction of the centre until exhaustion forced her to stop at a children's playground. She lay down on a graffiti covered bench beside the swings and fell into uneasy sleep until the sound of male laughter woke her as dawn was breaking. Two scruffy-looking teenage boys were leering at her and making obscene gestures. She got off the bench and ran; the boys' laughter finally fading in the distance. On a narrow pavement, an old woman struggled with a large bag of shopping and her walking stick. As Yasmin approached, the woman suddenly stepped off the pavement without looking into the path of a bicycle laden with simit, the ubiquitous Turkish bagels topped with sesame seeds.

The cyclist swerved abruptly but not in time to avoid colliding with the woman, sending her and her shopping sprawling. Yasmin bent down to help the woman back onto her feet while a little girl gathered up the fallen shopping. The woman and girl stared at Yasmin in disbelief before thanking this most unlikely helper, while the retreating cyclist hurled imprecations at pedestrians in general, elderly pedestrians and ragged pedestrians in particular. Left on her own again, Yasmin looked down and saw that a simit had fallen off the bike onto the kerb. Quick as a flash, she grabbed it and ran. It smelled delicious but she struggled to eat it, the bread refusing to succumb in her tinder-dry mouth.

The streets all looked the same—an endless crisscrossing of crowded corridors flanked by high apartment buildings preventing any chance of glimpsing well-known landmarks beyond the immediate vicinity. People stared as she made her way along the narrow streets. This was not a tourist area, and no one wore sleeveless tops and jeans, let alone filthy, ripped versions. No one else looked as if they had come off second best in a tussle with a wild animal. Some of the stares were expressionless but many were hostile, and Yasmin had never felt so out of place, so marginalised, so excluded from the society around her.

All along the street, shopkeepers had raised their metal shutters, congesting the already narrow pavements with displays of household goods, cheap shoes, fruit and vegetables and racks of clothes. Ahead of her, Yasmin watched as a woman struggled to release a sweater from a tightly packed rack knocking the whole thing over in the process. While the shopkeeper raged, Yasmin instinctively bent down to help the woman pick up the fallen clothes. As she did so, she noticed a pile of hijabs in a box behind the fallen rack. While the shop owner's attention was fixed on restoring order to his wares, Yasmin picked up a hijab and stuffed it under her top. The hijab would make her less noticeable in the crowds—survival was turning her into a very proficient thief.

Round a corner, a burst main spewed water all over the street. Throwing caution to the winds and oblivious to the scandalised looks of passers-by, Yasmin started scooping water into her hands, letting it dribble into her mouth and over her face and arms. Her right arm stung like mad. Eventually, she became aware of a crowd gathering around her and someone warning her not to drink the water. She didn't care. She felt dizzy as she rose to her feet. No one moved. No one spoke. She pushed her way past turning the first corner she came to and slumped on the pavement gasping for breath and waiting for the dizziness to pass.

Back on her feet, she continued along a street which ended at a major intersection controlled by traffic lights. Looking to her right, she saw a large, complicated road sign with directions to a host of destinations, none of which she recognised as she struggled to link written and phonic Turkish. Knowing virtually nothing of the layout of the city, or the names of its districts did not help matters but after five minutes of intense concentration, she recognised the sign for Sultanahmet—wasn't that where Hagia Sophia and the Blue Mosque were?

Arranging the generous folds of the hijab over her head and shoulders, she felt less conspicuous but as she walked on, she was aware that the buildings and shops were becoming smarter, people were more elegantly dressed and attractive cafés and restaurants lined fashionable squares. The looks she attracted were mainly of indifference or disdain and it occurred to her that heading for the centre might not be such a good idea after all. What would she do in the city centre anyway? — Ask for directions to the British Consulate. Looking as she did, she was more likely to get arrested than receive help.

Unsure what to do next, Yasmin turned off the main road onto a tree-lined side street. At the far end, a queue of people stood outside a mosque. Was it Friday? — She was no longer sure. As she got closer, she noticed that the people—mainly poorly dressed men—were waiting patiently at a long table where women were serving bowls of something that smelled delicious along with the ubiquitous flatbreads. She was so hungry, so exhausted and so past caring that she joined the queue. When her turn came, the woman handing over her food looked at her with concern and asked if she was all right. After a moment of indecision, Yasmin nodded assent and moved away. Her bowl contained a spicy tomato soup laced with beans and chickpeas. Nothing had ever tasted so delicious. When she handed back the empty bowl, she noticed that the woman who had served her was in deep discussion with another helper, and both glanced in her direction as they spoke. The second woman was tall, simply but elegantly dressed, and even at a distance, Yasmin could tell that she retained traces of what must have been a remarkable beauty in her youth.

Yasmin bolted. Maybe she had no right to be in that queue, no right to free food, and no right to be at the mosque. Slowing down at the next junction, she looked to her right along Meşrutiyet Cadesi, a broad street of affluent houses. Her legs almost gave out in relief at the sight of the British flag flying above a large, heavily guarded building set back from the road in substantial grounds. Two heavily armed guards stood outside a massive gate behind which she could see a reinforced, cube-like control room. A police or army SUV with radio antennae was parked alongside the perimeter wall. Above the gate was a familiar insignia and a discreet sign confirming that this was the Consulate General of Great Britain and Northern Ireland.

Summoning up her last reserves of courage, Yasmin approached one of the guards and said, "I am British, and I am in trouble. I need help"—immediately realising her mistake. She had spoken in Turkish, not English. How British did she appear? — Filthy dirty, wearing a hijab, Middle

Eastern skin colouring and speaking fluent Turkish. She looked like a local down-and-out.

"Do you have an appointment?"

"No, but I desperately need help."

"Best be on your way, miss. Phone for an appointment if you want to see someone."

"I can't phone—I have no money and my phone is out of charge."

"As I said, miss. Best be on your way!"—this time said more firmly, the gun raised a fraction.

Yasmin stood back, in tears and irresolute.

"On your way! NOW!"

She turned and left.

Yasmin retraced her steps to the relative anonymity of less opulent streets—back towards the mosque and the women who had served food. She would hand herself over to them. It no longer mattered how they responded—even arrest and imprisonment had to be better than this. A few more days on the streets without the skills to survive in the precarious world of the homeless; she knew she would die. The debilitating dizziness had returned, and she lost her way in the maze of streets and alleyways. By the time she found the mosque again, dusk had fallen. To her dismay, the compound was locked up for the night and there was no sign of anyone around. Defeated and ill, she limped around to the back of the building and slumped against the wall, unable to go any further. Her arm felt on fire and sweat had broken out on her brow even though the night air was cool.

If only she could think straight…but her mind seemed to be jumping from one hallucinatory image to another without making any sense. Then nothing. She was woken by a gentle tap on the shoulder, amazed to discover it was already daylight. Her arm still ached—in fact, most of her body ached—but she could think more clearly. A wizened old lady was looking down at her, concern etched on her face.

"You need to get up—you could be attacked or arrested if you stay here," she said, breaking off a piece of bread and handing it to her as she spoke.

"Do you have any water?" Yasmin asked.

The woman shook her head and turned away. To Yasmin's surprise, she returned a few minutes later with a bottle of water. Yasmin took it, spluttering tearful words of thanks through greedy gulps of water.

"You need to go to the mosque," the woman said as she turned away knowing that Yasmin's need for help was beyond any she could give.

Yasmin rose painfully and the world started spinning. Grabbing a railing, she waited until the dizziness passed before making her way slowly around to the main entrance to the mosque. The long table had been set up but there was no one in sight. The world started spinning again, then went dark. Indistinct voices broke into the fog inside her head, gentle hands under her arms helped her slowly back onto her feet, the same voices asking if she could walk—could she? She was led into a large room inside the compound and lowered onto some soft cushions. As her sight cleared, she recognised the woman who had served her the day before.

"What's your name?" The woman asked gently.

"Yasmin. Yasmin Cilic, but I am actually British." The effort of speaking made her head reel. "I'm—I'm in terrible trouble…"

The woman turned to a colleague and said, "I need to call Ayşe—she will know what to do about this."

"Will I get her something to eat meantime?" Someone asked.

"Best not—look at her arm. She needs hospital treatment and if that includes anaesthetic, her stomach needs to be empty. Just bring some water."

Even through the fog of fever, Yasmin smiled to herself— no problem with an empty stomach—it had never been so empty. In any case, she felt too sick to eat.

Twenty minutes later, the tall, beautiful woman she had seen the day before appeared. A compassionate smile lit her face as she introduced herself as Ayşe Demercol.

"Let's see what we can do to help. Would you mind if we start with some personal information?" Yasmin didn't notice the startled look on Ayse's face as she gave her name, address, date of birth and nationality.

"I'm in terrible trouble…" Yasmin started to say.

"Let's not worry about that right now. We need to get you to a doctor first, and then you can tell us what has happened to you."

"I haven't any money…but if you phone my father in Scotland, he'll send whatever you need."

"Don't worry about that. We'll sort everything out for you. Can you wait a moment while I make a couple of phone calls? Miriam will look out some clothes for you from a store we keep for emergencies."

Ayşe moved away to make the calls. From the little Yasmin could hear, the first was to a clinic to say that Yasmin would be brought in. The second call set off alarm bells. Yasmin distinctly heard Ayşe say, "I think we may have found the missing girl." Two days ago, she would have made a run for it, but she was too weak and too ill to care—resigned to whatever was to happen to her.

Miriam reappeared with a bundle of clean clothes while Ayşe went to collect her car. "Hardly the height of fashion," Miriam said apologetically, but better than the ones you are wearing. Yasmin emerged into the courtyard resplendent in a pair of Turkish trousers and a loose chemise. A clean bandage temporarily covered the angry gash in her arm. Gliding through the streets of Istanbul in the passenger seat of a large Audi felt surreal after days of rough living. Ayşe pulled up in front of an imposing clinic set back from the road in a lovely garden.

"I can't go into a clinic looking like this," Yasmin said, panic rising at the thought of the cost. Her father was not a rich man.

"It's all right, Yasmin. I have explained the situation to the director of the clinic."

They were met at the door by two nurses who led Yasmin into a well-equipped treatment room. After checking her temperature and blood pressure, they helped her undress and step into a shower, telling her to hold onto the grab rail in case she felt faint.

"We just want to get some of the dust off you so that the doctor can get a proper look at your injuries." Yasmin smiled at their tact. She knew she must also smell awful.

Yasmin could have lingered there forever, allowing the warm water to flow over her, but all too soon, it was switched off and a nurse appeared with a large white towelling robe. Back in the treatment room, the robe was removed, and she was helped onto a bed and covered with a blissfully clean sheet.

The nurses stood back deferentially as an imposing, middle-aged woman wearing a spotless white coat entered the room. Dark, intelligent eyes glinted behind heavily-rimmed glasses and her voice as she introduced herself to Yasmin was quiet and assured. An attempt had been made to capture most of her luxurious hair in an ornate silver grip from which several defiant strands escaped softening the overall severity of her appearance.

While her wounds were being cleaned and treated the doctor asked a stream of questions. 'How did you come by these injuries? Do you have a headache? Do you feel dizzy or nauseous? Is your sight affected? If I press your arm here, or here, on a scale of one to ten, how would you rate the pain?'

Yasmin skipped answering the first question, other than to state that her injuries had been caused by falling on rough ground after her passport and money had been stolen. All true, albeit a heavily redacted version of events. She answered 'yes' to all queries about symptoms and 'nine' to the question about pain level.

"You have cracked ribs, a high temperature and infection is spreading from the wound in your arm. You are also severely dehydrated. For all these reasons, we are going to keep you here for a day or two in the hope that complete rest, intravenous antibiotic, and a saline drip will work their magic. My colleagues will keep a close eye on your temperature and blood pressure, both of which are higher than they should be. Is there anything you would like to ask?"

"You have been very kind, but I can't possibly stay here. I don't have any money."

"It's all right. Mrs Demercol is sorting that out. I am leaving you now in the care of our excellent nursing staff and will see you again in the morning to check on your progress." With that, she left the room.

Yasmin groaned. She would have to ask her father to send money to repay Mrs Demercol—and how many months of work in a small restaurant would be needed to cover the cost of treatment in an upmarket clinic, but she was too exhausted to argue. Her father! She needed to phone him to tell him where she was—but her phone was out of charge, and it had been in the back pocket of the jeans she had left at the mosque. She sat up too quickly and her head spun—thoughts spilling over each other in a senseless tangle of worries.

Steadying arms held her until the dizziness passed and the nurses gently eased her off the bed onto a wheelchair. "We are going to take you to your room now and get you settled. I know Dr Orlova can seem rather gruff at times, but don't let that upset you. She is an excellent doctor and really cares about her patients."

She was taken to a bright room looking out over a garden. In addition to a bed, the room was furnished with a chest of drawers on top of which sat a television. A comfortable armchair and built-in wardrobes completed the furnishing. *Not that I have much need of a wardrobe at the moment*, she thought in a rare flash of her old sense of humour. A carafe of water sat on the bedside table and …her phone was connected to a charger! She started to cry as a nurse settled her into bed while her colleague explained how to call for assistance. She didn't notice the needle going into her arm, only the gentle drift into oblivion.

The next thing she was aware of was waking up in a comfortable bed, shafts of morning sunlight danced across the room and a delicious smell of warm bread made her mouth water. It was only when she tried to move that she realised she had drips in both arms. A different nurse was at her bedside, smiling as she arranged a breakfast tray—orange juice, Turkish tea in a glass beaker, yoghurt, bread and fruit. Yasmin was in heaven.

"We have let your family know that you are alive and recovering well, and your father intends to fly out as soon as possible. A policeman will be in to see you later this morning..." Seeing the look of panic on Yasmin's face, the nurse hastened to reassure her. "Don't be alarmed, it will be Mrs Demercol's husband, Commander Demercol. He is very nice, and I believe a Scottish policeman might be with him."

Don't be alarmed! Yasmin thought. *What possible reason could I have for being alarmed at the prospect of being interviewed by the Turkish police! I have no passport, no means of identity, no proof of how or when I arrived in Türkiye. I spent several weeks with drug dealers—my brother among them. Witnessed a shoot-out in which a policeman and some drug dealers were killed. I have no idea whether my brother is alive or dead. If he is alive, I have no idea where he might be. I could always add the theft of an apple and a hijab just to complete my criminal profile*! Maybe it was the effect of the drugs, but Yasmin felt surprisingly fatalistic about whatever was in store for her. *For now, I am going to concentrate on enjoying this breakfast. I doubt if prison fare will be as good.*

Chapter 23
Orhan

When their van ran out of fuel shortly after fleeing the crime scene, Orhan, Ulrich and Rafiq had no choice but to make for the hills on foot. They could hear police sirens getting dangerously close and a helicopter was sweeping backwards and forwards overhead. "We need to hide somewhere until nightfall," Ulrich said.

"Don't be daft," Rafiq replied. "As soon as they find the van, police will begin searching the nearby area with dogs. We need to get out of here."

"And how do you suggest we do that?" Orhan asked. "I doubt that a bus will trundle along any time soon to transport us all to freedom!"

"We need to hijack a car. It's the only way. Dispose of the driver to make sure news of the hijack doesn't reach the police too soon."

The basic problem with this plan was an absence of cars on the narrow country lane beside the ditch they were using as a temporary and not very effective hiding place. Eventually, a motorbike approached. Ulrich staggered out into the road forcing the rider to swerve abruptly. The rider fought and failed to bring the bike under control. It hit the bank on the far side of the road and rebounded before falling on its side, trapping the rider underneath. Pinned under the weight of his bike, his dispatch by Rafiq was swift. Righting the bike, Ulrich kicked the young man's body into the ditch.

A further problem with this plan was that Orhan was badly injured. A bullet was lodged in his hip and his initial hope, in the momentary anaesthesia which follows major injury, that it was just a graze faded as pain kicked in and an angry gash in his jeans revealed an even angrier gash underneath. The wound was bleeding profusely, and the ripped shirt used to stem the flow was saturated. Unable to walk unaided, a motorbike was no solution for him. It made the decision of whom to leave behind a simple one. Ulrich and Rafiq left without a backward glance. As evening fell, police dogs found Orhan lying unconscious alongside the body of a young Turkish man. It would be 24 hours before the police realised that the young man was a victim, not part of the gang.

It was the following morning before Orhan's condition was stable enough for him to be questioned by the police. During that time, he had concocted a version of events that he hoped would convince the Turkish police. 'While on holiday in Türkiye with his sister and friends, they got lost in Istanbul and found themselves near a derelict industrial site. As they attempted to phone for a taxi, they were surrounded by a gang of drug dealers who thought they were undercover police. They were taken to a disused warehouse; their passports and money were confiscated, and they were locked in. The gang leader, Rafiq, forced Orhan and his friends to sell drugs on the street, keeping his sister at the warehouse as hostage. They had been forced out of the warehouse at gunpoint when the police arrived but were not involved in the shoot-out—they didn't even have guns. He, Ulrich, and Rafiq took fright when they saw that a police officer had been killed and made off in the van. He had been too badly injured to go further when the van ran out of fuel and passed out due to loss of blood soon afterwards. He believed that Ulrich and Rafiq had left looking for help. He didn't know who the dead man found beside him was or how he came to be there. He didn't know what had happened to his sister. He hoped she was all right.'

Orhan was rather pleased with this ingenious re-imagining of the story. That was until he saw a very senior Turkish police officer talking to the armed guard outside his room, and a man in civilian clothes standing right behind him. A man whose face he recognised from extensive news coverage of a series of murders linked to international art theft. A man whose name was all too well-known inside Scotland's criminal fraternity. A man who might know far too much about the circumstances surrounding the death of Hafez Yilmaz. A man who would know Orhan had not been holidaying in Türkiye. A man who was supposed to have retired from the police force. Arbuthnot! As the two men entered his room, Orhan felt his world fall apart, barely noticing the slim, young man following in their wake.

"Mr Cilic, I am Commander Demercol of the Istanbul Serious Crimes Directorate, and my colleague is former Superintendent John Arbuthnot representing the interests of two Scottish police forces, Lothian and Borders, and Tayside."

"I know who Arbuthnot is. Thought you'd retired!"

"Life is full of disappointments, Mr Cilic," Arbuthnot replied with a hint of a smile. "Once the Turkish authorities have finished with you—which I imagine will not be for some considerable time—I can guarantee that you will have plenty opportunities to meet serving police officers in Scotland."

Demercol resumed the lead, "The gentleman behind me is defence lawyer, Mr David Inönü, who will represent your interests at this interview. The interview will be conducted in English and recorded."

"For the record: earlier today, you were formally charged by one of my colleagues with two offences: possession of illegal substances with intention to sell; and holding your sister hostage in Bodrum and Istanbul. Please confirm that you understand the charges."

"I was forced to sell the drugs by a Turkish gang, and I was held hostage too."

"You will have plenty time to answer these charges in a courtroom. For the moment, I just need you to confirm that you understand the charges." Orhan looked across at Inönü who nodded.

"I understand, but I deny them both."

"Moving on, I also want to interview you in connection with the death of one of my police officers and the death of Mr Năzim Shafak whose body was found beside you yesterday."

"Wait a minute! I didn't kill anyone!"

"All in good time, Mr Cilic. All in good time," Demercol said. "I just wish we also had a law against abandoning a sister in a strange city without the means to find shelter, food or support. But I *will* include the theft of her passport and credit cards in the list of charges against you."

Orhan maintained a sullen silence. He had noticed that the superficial charm of the Commander did not reach his eyes. Arbuthnot's stare was equally uncompromising as he added,

"You must be very concerned about your sister, Mr Cilic. Good Heavens, we haven't given you the chance to ask whether she is dead or alive, safe or in grave danger. You must be out of your mind with worry—But more for what she might tell us than for her wellbeing would be my guess."

Orhan remembered what was said on the streets of Edinburgh—Arbuthnot was seriously bad news.

"You will be pleased to know that your sister is in hospital being treated for several injuries, none of them life-threatening thankfully, and she is making good progress. Such good progress, in fact, that we will be able to interview her later today."

Demercol took up the thread, "The truth is, Mr Cilic, we hardly know where to start. It is evident that some very serious crimes committed in Scotland are closely linked to very serious crimes committed in Istanbul, two of which have already led to formal charges against you. These and any further charges against you for crimes committed in Türkiye will be subject to Turkish law and heard in a Turkish Court. Do you understand?"

Orhan looked anxiously at Inönü, who nodded.

"I understand but I deny everything. I am the victim here!"

"Two senior Scottish detectives will be here shortly to interview you formally in connection with crimes committed in Scotland. However, to fully understand what has happened in Türkiye, we need to know more about the events which prompted your precipitate flight to Bodrum, specifically your role in the trafficking of minors into Scotland, leading to the disappearance and death of a Turkish citizen, Dr Hafez

Yilmaz, and the kidnap and abduction of your sister Yasmin Cilic."

Arbuthnot heard the catch in Kadir's voice as he mentioned the young doctor. Kadir had not forgiven himself for failing to realise how obsessively reckless Hafez had become since the murder of his wife, Amara. Hafez was the son of close friends of the Demercol family, and it had been Kadir who had asked him to pass on any information about migrant routes he *happened to hear* in the course of his work at the Cordari Clinic. He had told Hafez to listen but not to draw attention to himself by asking questions. Hafez had paid a very high price for ignoring that advice.

John took the lead again to give Kadir a moment to collect himself, heading off another indignant outburst from Orhan.

"Before you try telling us you were taking Yasmin on a holiday that ended badly, we have evidence to prove that Yasmin had other holiday plans for the dates in question. Added to which, there are members of staff at Edinburgh Airport—at check-in, security, and departures, who live with regret at failing to pick up on Yasmin's distress."

Demercol picked up the thread again.

"You told my colleagues you were betrayed by relatives in Bodrum, taken against your will to Istanbul and forced to work for a drug gang. I have a simple question to ask about that. Why didn't you use one of the burner phones you were supplied with for 'business purposes' to call the British Consulate or the police to explain your predicament? I'll leave that question hanging for the moment. Let's start at the beginning, shall we—with the trafficking of underage Romanian girls on behalf of one of the Manson brothers…"

Chapter 24
The Orlov Clinic Istanbul
June 1997

Set in tranquil gardens overlooking the Bosphorus, the Orlov Clinic had provided excellent health care for its wealthy clients since 1918. Its founder, Dr Antonin Orlov, had fled revolutionary Russia and since then, three generations of the family had followed in his footsteps. The main building was a traditional, Turkish mansion house modernised over the years to provide a high standard of state-of-the-art health care. The current director, Dr Valentina Orlova, was admired rather than loved by her staff who did their best to meet her exacting standards. She was adored by her patients once they realised her bark was infinitely worse than her bite.

It was late afternoon when the door to Yasmin's room opened, and two men entered. Yasmin's heart skipped a beat. The police! Although she had been warned they were coming and had been reassured that there was nothing to be alarmed about, she was alarmed. Instinctively, she drew herself up into sitting position, swept her hair back from her face and attempted a nervous smile. None of this did anything to calm her jangling nerves. One of the detectives approached her bed and addressed her in polished Turkish—the kind of Turkish she had only heard in her mother's favourite film—a murder mystery set in the luxurious Pera Palace Hotel. Embarrassed at the prospect of responding in the rough dialect she had learned at her mother's knee, she breathed a sigh of relief when the elegant man who had introduced himself as Commander Kadir Demercol switched to equally polished English to introduce his companion, former Superintendent John Arbuthnot representing the interests of the Scottish police.

"If you feel ready, we would just like to know how and why you came to Türkiye; and about everything that has happened since you arrived here."

"I don't really understand much of it, but the day after my twenty-first birthday party, my brother Orhan Cilic was in a rage, insisting that he had to leave Scotland and forcing me to go with him, even though I was supposed to be going on holiday with a friend that day. He had taken my passport and money and my attempts at check-in, security, and departure to alert staff to the fact that I was being taken abroad against my will came to nothing. He said we were going to stay with relatives in Bodrum—relatives I had never heard of. We were clearly not welcome and they sent us on to Istanbul…"

"Why do you think your brother was so anxious to escape from Scotland?"

"I don't really know. It may have been because he thought a friend of mine had been spying on him at my party and before that at my parents' restaurant in Dundee. Orhan was always mixed up in things he shouldn't have been…"

"What sort of things?"

"I don't know. Things that enabled him to live in a big house and drive flashy cars. We were all afraid of him—my parents especially, and he surrounded himself with some very unpleasant characters. We didn't ask questions—I suppose we were afraid of the answers."

"But the friend you invited to your party had started to ask questions?"

"If he did, he didn't tell me."

"What was your friend's name?"

Yasmin's expression softened, "Hafez, Hafez Yilmaz. He is a doctor doing some research at Dundee University. He is a lovely man. He came to my party even though it wasn't really his thing—drinking and dancing, that is. He left early to get back to Dundee—the party was at Orhan's club in Edinburgh, so he had a long journey home."

Kadir and John looked at each other—both had noticed Yasmin's use of the present tense in talking about Hafez.

"Did you hear from Dr Yilmaz after he left the party?"

"No, I texted him twice, but he didn't reply, then I was dragged off to Bodrum by Orhan and my phone ran out of charge. I haven't heard from him since."

The regret in her voice was undeniable.

John Arbuthnot took over. "Yasmin, I'm afraid we have some very sad news for you. Dr Yilmaz is dead—he was murdered."

"Murdered! How? What happened? Don't tell me it was Orhan!" Yasmin collapsed back onto her pillows sobbing quietly. Almost immediately, she raised herself up again, "If it was that bastard, I'll kill him myself! Tell me what happened, please."

"I think you need a break—I'll call for some tea."

"No, no break—please, tell me what happened to Hafez." They told her.

Yasmin lay back, closing her eyes. Her face was as white as the pillows supporting her head.

"Is Orhan still alive?"

"Yes, he's still alive and under arrest."

"Good. Now let me tell you the rest of the story and I hope it is enough to ensure he is in prison for the rest of his miserable life. I no longer have a brother!"

Chapter 25
Ulrich

Ulrich sat on a bench in a run-down area on the outskirts of the ancient university city of Eskişehir. Not that Ulrich knew that the city was either ancient or a seat of learning. All he knew was that it provided a bench on which to contemplate his future. He was exhausted following the 330km ride south on a bike designed for urban commuting not for long-distance travel. It was time to take stock of his situation and there was no escaping the fact that his situation was grim. Early that morning, he had left Rafiq to face his destiny in a village the name of which he neither knew nor wanted to know.

Rafiq had attempted to shoplift food and cigarettes from the village store. As commotion broke out in the shop, Ulrich had ridden off at top speed, not stopping until he reached the bench on which he was now considering his options. None held much promise. He had to get out of Türkiye where he was wanted in connection with at least two murders, drug dealing and the theft of a motorbike—the battered motorbike currently propped up beside him, its travelling days at an end. The question was where to go and how to get there. He couldn't go back to Scotland where he was wanted in connection with the death of Hafez Yilmaz, drug dealing, and people trafficking. He didn't have the resources to get to far-flung boltholes in Asia or South America.

Despite his German name, he had no connection with the German-speaking world. He was the result of a brief fling his Scottish mother had had with an Austrian student whose surname and contact details she had omitted to obtain. He was named after the father his mother hardly knew, brought up in the troubled Muirhouse area of Edinburgh, and educated from time to time at Craigroyston High School. A successful early career as a bouncer at *The Marmaris* in Edinburgh had landed him the job as chief bodyguard and enforcer for Orhan Cilic.

Foremost among his immediate difficulties was his appearance. Ulrich was over six feet tall and heavily built. His light brown beard did not conceal the pale skin, blue eyes, and Germanic set of his large head. Melting into the crowds in a Middle Eastern country was never going to be easy. He had two passports, but to use either would be suicidal. His British passport was genuine, issued in the name of Ulrich McGurk and guaranteed to raise a security alert at any airport, seaport, or land crossing where it was presented. The second passport was Austrian, in the name of Ulrich Reinhardt, and forged. The trouble was that Ulrich spoke no German and had never been to Austria. A further problem was that Turkish Immigration would have no record of an Ulrich Reinhardt entering the country, leading to all sorts of uncomfortable questions about how he came to be leaving it. The priority was to get out of Türkiye, the choice of destination would have to wait.

Ever alert to escape possibilities during his drug-dealing days in Istanbul, Ulrich had befriended the youngest and brightest of their captors, a young tear-away aged about fifteen. To talk of escape routes would have led to serious trouble, so Ulrich simply asked the lad to tell him about Türkiye and learned that it stretched from the north where the lad thought it bordered Greece or maybe Bulgaria at a place called 'Erdny' (Edirne). He didn't know what Bulgaria was like, but the Greeks were apparently a bad lot. Then there was the Black Sea to the east of Istanbul with countries like Russia and Ukraine somewhere around there—the lad had looked doubtful for a moment as if questioning the accuracy of what he was saying.

Ulrich had already discounted the Black Sea option, getting into any country on its north shore might be a lot easier than getting out again. To the south, Türkiye went on for thousands of kilometres—it was as big as Russia or America according to the lad who had no idea what lay beyond its southern borders, maybe Egypt or Syria or somewhere like that. Ulrich had thanked him for the geography 'lesson.'

He knew it had been a mistake to travel south, but his only thought during the escape from Istanbul had been to put as much distance as possible between himself and the police. Heading south had been the fastest route out of the city. Now he was stuck in the vastness of central Türkiye with no idea where to go next. Along his escape route, he had seen signs for a place called Izmir. Izmir had received no mention during his recent geography lesson, but he had noticed a ship depicted on a direction sign indicating that Izmir might be a port. He had also noticed that it was about 500km to the west of Eskişehir. He doubted if either he or the bike could make it that far.

He had very little money. Well, that was not strictly true, but most of it was in sterling. Trying to use it or exchange it would draw unwanted attention. He had a credit card, to be accurate a card in the name of Hafez Yilmaz, linked to an account with the Banco di Sicilia. Before dumping Hafez's body overboard, he had been unable to resist looking in Hafez's wallet. He had four cards, two for different accounts at the Merkez Bankasi—presumably a Turkish bank, one Bank of Scotland card, and a card for an account with the Banco di Sicilia. The first three would be unusable, but he had decided to keep the Sicilian card—maybe news of Hafez's death might not have reached the Banco di Sicilia. Unfortunately, the contents of the wallet did not include a useful note of the pin number.

He needed to get to the coast—maybe he should head towards this Izmir place, though if it was important enough to be flagged up 500 kilometres away it must be big. If it turned out to be a large port, that would mean tight controls, but maybe from there he could go up or down the coast a bit and find a way to get off the mainland.

Across the road was a service station where he could get fuel for the bike, but the bike was not up to a long journey over who knew what kind of terrain. The service station had a shop and a small café where three men sat cradling glasses of tea. They were shortly joined by a fourth who had just left his three-wheeled truck in the parking lot—a parking lot which was visible from Ulrich's vantage point, but not from the café. Ulrich sauntered over to the truck. It was open at the back with traces of fresh vegetables on the metal floor suggesting that it had just been on a market run. Best of all, the key was in the ignition. Vehicle theft was obviously not an issue in this part of Eskişehir. At least it hadn't been till now.

The first thing Ulrich noticed when he switched on the engine was that the fuel gauge was registering empty, and a red light was flashing on the dashboard. He couldn't refuel at this service station as the pumps were in full view of the café—he had to hope that another service station would appear before the fuel ran out completely and before the police were informed of the theft and service stations put on the alert.

Chapter 26
Pera Palace Hotel, Istanbul
June 1997

"I keep expecting to see Agatha Christie or Ernest Hemingway appearing through a doorway," Anya remarked as she surveyed the magnificent chandeliers, mirrors, and belle epoque furnishings of the legendary Pera Palace Hotel. Ayşe had suggested going for coffee in the fabulous Kubbeli lounge, followed by a tour of the hotel's most famous rooms, in one of which Agatha Christie was said to have written *Murder on the Orient Express*. She is rumoured to have hidden here during her mysterious 11-day disappearance, but whether that is true or not is anyone's guess. The one thing you can be sure of is that if a guest asks the Pera Palace to say nothing about their presence, nothing will be said!

"We can also visit the room where Kemal Atatürk, founder of the Turkish Republic, stayed in the aftermath of World War I. His room is now a museum." Coffee and tour merged predictably into lunch, neither woman in a hurry to leave the timeless beauty and tranquillity of this iconic place to reengage with the hustle and bustle of the city.

"I sometimes wonder if you and I will ever enjoy a proper holiday with our husbands without some major crime getting in the way," Anya mused as she contemplated the ruins of their projected tour of less-trodden parts of Türkiye.

"I was thinking exactly the same thing," Ayşe replied, setting down her wine glass and gazing pensively out of the window at the dappled sunshine on the Orient Terrace. "You already know Istanbul well, so why don't we go somewhere else for a few days while our husbands are busy interviewing murderers and drug dealers, searching for escaping gangsters, and questioning victims."

"Excellent idea," said Anya. "Where shall we go?"

"Have you ever been to Izmir, old Smyrna that is? It is a fascinating city which has survived fire and earthquakes, not to mention ravages by Romans, Crusaders, Seljuq Turks, Tamerlane, and the Greeks. Alexander the Great is said to have founded a second city over the ruins of the first, attracted by its sheltered harbour. We could visit the Agora of ancient Smyrna and the archaeological site Bayrakli Höyüğu. There is an amazing clock tower in the central square designed by Charles Perrin, and the famous Kemaralti market where you can buy just about anything. On the way to Izmir, we could also visit Pergamum if you like."

"Let's do it!" was the response.

*

They set off very early next morning, stopping for a late lunch at a roadside café on the Kozak Plain. Majestic pine trees towered overhead, their vibrant crowns reaching towards a cloudless sky. A light breeze played on the lower branches casting shimmering shadows onto the road below.

"You see where Türkiye's famous pine nuts come from," the waiter said waving his arm in a theatrical gesture in the direction of a line of trees. "I recommend the biber dolmasi (stuffed peppers) made by my wife this morning. From the very first bite, you will taste how wonderful our pine nuts are." He wasn't wrong. The delicious flavours of onion, tomato and spice infused the rice, setting off the crisp, almost sweet taste of the roasted pine nuts against the sharpness of green pepper. After lunch, they took a short stroll along a tree-lined path, the air redolent with the scent of pine resin.

Back in their car for the final 20 kilometres to Pergamum, Anya's attention was caught by the sight of a man tinkering with the engine of a three-wheeled truck at the roadside. Nothing unusual about that, but something about the man seemed out of place, stirring a recollection she could not retrieve.

"Did you see that man fixing his truck?"

"Briefly. I'm too busy concentrating on the traffic to notice much else."

"He didn't look like a local."

Ayşe laughed, "I'm not sure what a 'local' looks like in this part of Türkiye given that armies from every nation on earth have swept over the place since time began, leaving little but DNA and destruction in their wake."

"Hm. It's probably nothing…he just seemed out of place."

The man and his truck were forgotten as their destination came into view. The ancient stones of Pergamum glowed in the late afternoon sunshine as Anya and Ayşe walked around marvelling at the sheer size of the ruined amphitheatre which once looked out over the distant Aegean, and at the remains of the magnificent temples to Athena and Dionysus. They talked at length about the rights and wrongs of the removal of the ancient friezes from the Altar of Zeus to Berlin, accepting that they might have been lost to posterity otherwise, but sad that they were no longer where they once belonged. As daylight faded, they set off for the adjacent modern city of Bergama and the historic Hera Hotel overlooking the Acropolis.

The next morning, they were reluctant to start out for Izmir immediately, so they left the car in a car park in the centre of town and set off to wander through its fabled back streets. It was like stepping back in time. Quaint buildings crowded along the narrow, cobbled streets. A few houses had been beautifully restored with windows and doors displaying intricate wrought iron work. The facing on others had long since given up the struggle against wild winter weather and the relentless summer sun, but there was a timeless charm in the faded colours, peeling plaster and curiously shaped windows and doors. Cats and dogs dozed on doorsteps or windowsills, barely raising their heads to look at passers-by. A few elderly women stood in doorways watching children play and variously welcoming or ignoring outsiders passing by. The streets were blissfully traffic-free apart from the occasional scooter or little three-wheeled van—the Ape (wasp) favoured throughout the Mediterranean for its ability to navigate the impossibly narrow streets and steep inclines of ancient towns and villages on Mediterranean and Aegean shores.

The first thing Anya noticed when they returned to the car park was the battered truck they had seen on the way into

Bergama. The driver had obviously managed to fix whatever problem had arisen the day before. The second thing she noticed was that there was no parking ticket attached to the dust-covered windscreen. Distracted for reasons she couldn't fathom, she failed to notice a white car being driven at speed towards her and it was only thanks to Ayşe's quick reaction that she wasn't run over.

Ayşe got a good look at the driver's face as the car sped towards them—it was the man they had seen yesterday, only he wasn't driving a battered truck; he was driving a Mercedes. In the fraction of a second it took for the car to pass them, both noticed the face of a terrified young woman in the passenger seat mouthing 'yardim!'—help! Neither managed to note the number plate as the car sped out of the car park onto the main road.

"I know who he is!"

"Who?"

"When Kadir and John were studying photographs on the table at your house two days ago, his was one of them. He is one of the men they are looking for in the Cilic case!"

Ayşe already had her phone clasped to her ear. Anya could hear Kadir's voice insisting that he would alert the local police, and that under NO circumstances should she and Anya attempt to follow the Mercedes. If the driver was indeed Ulrich, he was very, very dangerous and wouldn't think twice about killing anyone who got in his way. Anya's phone rang as Kadir was talking. It was John, giving her the same, unequivocal message. The calls cut off simultaneously.

"By the time the local police get their act together, Ulrich could be miles away in any one of several directions," Anya said. Without another word, they both started running towards their car.

"We can follow at a safe distance. That way we can at least tell the police where to start looking for him. It looks as if he is heading north and the traffic between here and the outskirts of town will be heavy, so with luck, we may catch sight of him."

*

The point of Ulrich's knife never left the side of the terrified woman beside him. The woman he had accosted as she approached her car, forcing her into the passenger seat and making her fasten the safety belt—not to save her from injury, but to impede any attempt to jump out of the car. Once in the driver's seat, he pressed central locking before moving off at speed. He was thankful that the car was an automatic, freeing his right hand to maintain the pressure of the knife point against his victim's side. Speeding towards the car park exit, there was a heart-stopping moment when a stupid woman stood in his way before being pulled back by her friend. Not that killing her would have bothered him, but it could have slowed down his departure and led to all sorts of complications he could well do without. The friend did bother him though. She had been staring at the car and at him as if she recognised him. Impossible, he knew, but for some reason warning bells were ringing.

Further frustrations awaited on the main road out of town. Traffic was very heavy, and anyone would think there had been a cheap sale of traffic lights—all of them at red. The last thing he needed was to be pulled over for a traffic violation, so he had to control his frustration until he reached the open road north towards the village of Dikili. A tourist office window in Bergama had displayed colourful posters in English about boat tours from Dikili, and a small boat with few passengers aboard setting off on a tour of the coastline was just what he needed. It was a pity the truck had finally given up the ghost and he had been forced to steal a car complete with its owner. But perhaps a hostage could come in useful if things got tricky and he needed a bargaining tool. If all went well, he would just get rid of her overboard. After all, it wouldn't be the first time he had disposed of someone overboard.

He drove around Dikili looking for a place to hide the Mercedes, wishing he had been able to steal a less conspicuous car, the theft of which was less likely to come to the attention of the police. In the end, he decided to leave the car in Otopark, a commercial car park near the shore hoping that it would remain hidden in plain sight among other cars until an attendant noticed that it had outstayed the maximum parking time. He threw away the unpaid ticket and car key in the nearest bin. The woman was seriously hampering his progress. He had momentarily thought of knocking her out and locking her into the boot of the car but quickly dismissed the idea. She might come around sooner rather than later and start creating a fuss.

He contemplated killing her, but a body slumped in a passenger seat would quickly come to someone's attention, and he couldn't carry a dead body around to the boot of the car in broad daylight in a public car park without being seen, so he had no option but to take her with him, the knife in his right-hand pocket pressed firmly into her side. Fear was keeping her reasonably docile, but he knew she would be looking for any opportunity to draw attention to her situation. Her shoes were both a blessing and a curse; a blessing in that the fashionably high heels and delicate straps were not conducive to running for her life. A curse in that they were never meant for walking any distance and her frequent stumbling set his nerves on edge.

Chapter 27
The Boat to Lesbos

Every few yards along the seafront, Ulrich was approached by people trying to sell tickets for boat trips along the coast, boat trips around the islands, luxury boat trips offering lunch and 'genuine' Turkish entertainment. All involved larger vessels with radio antennae and room for far too many passengers. Alongside these vessels, a few fishing boats rode at anchor, but these too had radio antennae and the men he could see working on deck looked more than capable of looking after themselves. This was not what he was looking for. The shoreline was too crowded and the constant wriggling and stumbling of his unwilling captive was playing havoc with his nerves.

Ulrich had always operated on a very short fuse, aggression frequently winning out over common sense, and in response to rising anger, he allowed his knife to pierce the layers of clothing between them and graze his captive's skin. Her loud gasp drew several concerned glances from passers-by, but most looking at the large angry man and his small, scared companion put it down to a 'domestic' and walked on, anxious not to get involved. Ulrich knew his luck could not hold out. He was so stressed that he did not notice a large white car cruising at a walking pace not far behind him.

"We've seen him. He's on the shore at Dikili looking at boats. He's got the woman with him."

Kadir's response to this information conveyed by his beloved wife was volcanic, ending with, "What part of DO NOT follow him did you not understand?"

Anya's phone was ringing so loudly that Ayşe could hardly hear what Kadir was saying. Reluctantly, Anya accepted the call and the rocketing that followed, ending with, "Kadir is on the phone to the local police who will take the matter on from here. You and Ayşe have done enough. *Go back* to your hotel in Bergama and we'll catch up with you there. We have just landed at Izmir Airport and a police escort is waiting for us."

*

The heel of one of his captive's shoes snapped off as she lost her footing on rough ground. In a rage, Ulrich yanked her to her feet and told her to 'take those fucking shoes off.' Weeping hysterically, she did as she was told, to be rewarded with a resounding slap across the face. 'Shut the fuck up and get walking.' Further, along the path, the commercial tour offers petered out to be replaced by hand-written offers in Turkish and something approximating English. The owners of two small craft sat along a crumbling pier smoking and chatting, waiting for customers who wanted an 'individual, competitively priced excursion'. An individual excursion was exactly what Ulrich had in mind. An excursion that would end near the Greek island of Lesbos with only one person left on board.

Ömar was relieved that it was his younger brother Mehmet's turn to take the passengers hurrying towards their pier. He didn't like the look of them at all—a huge, angry-looking foreign man pushing his terrified partner down the steep steps towards the boats. As he helped the woman onto Mehmet's boat, he noticed that she wore no shoes and her feet were bleeding. The man was arguing threateningly with Mehmet in what sounded like English. Ömar had skipped so many English lessons at school that he had to rely on his brother when it came to dealing with foreign customers, but there was no doubt about the look of desperation in his brother's eyes as he cast off. Ömar didn't know what to do. What could he tell the police? — That his brother had agreed to take two dodgy-looking customers out to Lesbos and seemed scared. He could imagine the response! There was also a small matter of their non-existent licence to ferry passengers to be considered before drawing the attention of the authorities to their activity.

A white car pulled up on the roadside above the pier and two women came hurtling down the steps towards a startled Ömar, still in a paralysis of indecision about his brother.

"You need to take us out to follow that boat. Right now, please!" Ömar stared in confusion at the tall, imposing woman who was already stepping into his boat, followed by her equally anxious-looking companion. This had to be the strangest day ever, and whoever these crazy women were, they made Ömar's mind up for him. He would follow his brother's boat and try to help him. Casting off, he wondered what on earth he had got himself into. The two women were staring ahead with an intensity that would have been almost frightening if they hadn't been so polite to him despite their obvious desperation to reach his brother's boat.

"Are you friends of the lady on the other boat?"

"Yes," was the terse reply.

"Do you think she is in danger?" He asked—superfluously.

"Yes."

At this point, Ömar seriously considered turning back, unwilling to get caught up in what could be a very nasty confrontation—then he remembered his brother, and reluctantly pointed the prow of his boat in the direction of Lesbos.

"Can't you go any faster?" Ömar turned to look at the taller of the two women. "Was she Turkish?" She certainly spoke elegant Turkish with the kind of accent he heard only on television, but she also spoke English—he thought—to her companion who looked foreign. Americans no doubt.

"Not safely," he replied, "there's quite a swell building up and we don't want to capsize." In fact, a darkening sky and strengthening wind were adding significantly to his concern about the wisdom of this expedition. Then he remembered his brother and casting caution aside, increased speed to maximum. Water cascaded over the boat and its uncomplaining passengers, but they were closing in on the other vessel. Ömar's boat was the more powerful of the two and Mehmet was making no attempt to evade his pursuers. Suddenly Ulrich stood up causing Mehmet's boat to roll precariously and before their horrified eyes, dragged the woman to her feet and threw her overboard. She wore no life vest. It took Anya a frozen moment to realise that neither of the boatmen made a move, remembering something she had once heard, that many sailors and fishermen did not swim, preferring a swift death by drowning to a prolonged struggle in the water before the inevitable. She knew Ayşe couldn't swim. In a flash, she kicked off her shoes and dived in. She was a strong swimmer, but it was slow going through the rough water.

Ömar followed at a safe distance to avoid adding to the turbulence around her. Anya had almost given up the frantic search when she realised what she had thought was seaweed was long hair splayed out across the surface of the water. She flipped over onto her back, grabbed hold of a handful of hair and pulled the woman's body back up to the surface and into the life-saving position. The freshening wind ruffled the waves sending sprays of icy water over their faces, temporarily blinding Anya, invading her mouth and nostrils and causing her to splutter. She struggled to keep the woman afloat, her dead weight threatening to drag both downwards. A large swell created by Ömar's boat coming alongside briefly submerged Anya, forcing her to release her hold on the woman as she struggled to clear her airways. In mounting panic she resurfaced, looking wildly around for any sign of the woman she was trying to save, and then she felt strong arms pulling her back into the boat. Ömar leant back over the side and caught the drowning woman by her hair. With Ayşe's help, he pulled her alongside.

"If I raise her head, can you lean over and grip her under one of her armpits?"

Ayşe managed to get hold of an arm, but as she did, the boat heeled over alarmingly; all the weight concentrated on one side.

"Get over to the other side," Ömar shouted at Anya who was doubled up on the decking coughing and spluttering, unable to do any more to help the drowned or drowning woman.

The boat steadied and Ömar swiftly shifted his grip from the woman's head to her other arm. Together they pulled slowly as the boat rocked wildly from side to side, landing the woman heavily on the decking.

With a quick glance to make sure that her friend was out of danger, Ayşe turned her attention to the woman she had saved and began administering CPD. With no response after an agonising and exhausting ten minutes, she was on the point of giving up when her efforts were suddenly rewarded by a spectacular burst of retching. As the bout subsided, the woman's eyes opened wide in terror, her panic-stricken gaze flitting over her new captors.

"What is your name?"

"mm—Miriam," was the faint response.

"Welcome back to life, Miriam," Ayşe said reaching out to stroke her face.

They were all soaking wet and frozen to the bone. Miriam was shivering uncontrollably, and they had nothing dry and warm to cover her with. The women's relief as a coastguard vessel approached their flimsy craft was not shared by Ömar who viewed the inevitable encounter with officialdom with mounting trepidation. Suddenly an authoritative voice cut through the sound of wind and waves. Through the spray and incipient rain, they could make out a man with a loudhailer on the deck of the fast-approaching vessel.

"We are coming alongside, stay where you are! We are going to transfer you to this vessel. If anyone is injured, can you wave—once for each injured person?"

As the transfer was about to take place, Ömar pushed the women to the side of the boat and started to rev the engine in preparation for a swift escape as soon as his passengers had been transferred.

"Boatman, switch off your engine NOW! We are to transfer you and tow your boat back to the harbour. These orders come from the police."

On board the coastguard vessel, they were given hypothermia wraps and mugs of strong, sweet Turkish tea. As the aroma of cinnamon and ginger gradually dispersed the harsh saline smell of seawater, and the warmth of tea flooded her system, Anya began to recover, and with recovery came the realisation of just how much danger they had been in only a few minutes earlier. She and Ayşe were in so much trouble! Miriam was hugging Ayşe as if her life depended upon it—and perhaps it was as shock set in.

Ömar sat hunched over his tea and on the verge of tears. He too was in serious trouble—trouble none of the women he had saved could possibly understand. At the very least, he and Mehmet would be charged with providing ferry services without a licence, without the relevant safety checks or safety equipment on board, and for operating without proper official documentation—or any sort of documentation for that matter. The small amount of money he and his brother made during the tourist season was all their family had to live on. Now their boats would be confiscated, and they could even end up with a prison sentence.

As the police launches closed in on Mehmet's boat, Ulrich attempted to push Mehmet over the side in the hope that the police would divert their efforts to searching for the man overboard. However, Mehmet was not as easy to push around as the woman had been and a struggle ensued during which the boat capsized throwing both into the water. Ulrich struck out strongly for the coast of Lesbos, but as he neared the island, the figures he had taken for happy holidaymakers enjoying a day on the beach, transpired to be an altogether less attractive group of people. A detachment of Greek border guards, two police frogmen and two mean-looking Alsatians made up this welcome party. A Greek police patrol launch lay idling at a nearby pier.

As Ulrich faced his final moments of freedom, he was in tears of rage at the injustice of it all. "That young gangster in Istanbul told me the Turks don't speak to the Greeks!"

Unfortunately, Ulrich's poor grasp of realpolitik had proved his undoing. Although diplomatic relations between the two nations veered between strained and very strained in the 1990s, in the world of policing, pragmatism ruled. The Turkish police wanted this man to face charges of murder, drug dealing and kidnap on Turkish soil. The Greek police did not want the criminal fraternity in Greece enriched by the kind of expertise a man like Ulrich might bring. The Greek Interior Ministry and criminal justice system would not thank the police for giving them the headache of detaining the man and dealing with the political minefield of jurisdiction that would follow—to say nothing of the expense of incarcerating him.

To complicate matters further, the Scottish police also wanted this man! All it had taken was a quiet phone call. Thus, to keep everyone happy—with the notable exception of

Ulrich—the obvious solution was to discourage Ulrich from swimming onto a Greek beach while turning a blind eye to two Turkish police launches which might or might not have entered Greek waters.

As the coastguard vessel approached land, the captain said he needed to record everyone's name and contact details. Miriam had only got as far as giving her surname 'Stavlakis' before the captain's eyes widened in astonishment and Ayşe interjected, "Stavlakis—the shipping magnate?"

"Yes," was the weary reply. "Nicos Stavlakis is my husband."

A short, thick-set man was pacing up and down the pier as the vessel tied up. He was middle-aged, elegantly dressed and clearly agitated. A new Jaguar XJ8 was parked at the quayside. A liveried driver stood by the door, his imposing height and powerful physique suggesting that he possessed all the additional skills necessary for ensuring the safety of a very high-value patron.

"It's Nicos," Miriam said in a tone of resignation. "He will be furious with me. I'm not supposed to go out without Iannis our driver, but sometimes I just like the freedom of being out on my own—at least I did until this morning."

As the gangplank lowered, Stavlakis raced up it, grabbed Miriam in a brief bear-like hug and made to head back down the gangplank with her.

"Wait, the police want to—" The captain's words were cut short.

"My wife is in no condition to answer questions just now! The police can call at my villa at 2 p.m. tomorrow afternoon. They know where it is."

With that and a cursory word of thanks to her rescuers, the magnate whisked his wife off to the waiting car.

As the jaguar pulled away from the quayside, two police cars drew up. Ömar instinctively knew the second, smaller car would be for him, and his destination would not be a grand villa in Izmir.

"A Jaguar would have been nice," Anya remarked, with a wry smile.

"That's the trouble with our men," Ayşe replied. "No imagination!"

As she spoke, Detective Chief Inspector Djavid could be seen racing down the steps towards the coastguard vessel, his face a picture of worry. As Commander Demercol's second-in-command, he was all too aware of just how much rested on getting the initial contact with his boss's wife right, not to mention getting her to comply with the very clear instructions he had been given. And from what he had seen of the Scottish policeman's wife, she was unlikely to be any easier to persuade.

"Here comes the cavalry," Ayşe said with a grimace.

"Are you both all right? Oh, my goodness! What on earth were you thinking of? You could have been killed!" Djavid's words spilt out in confused order as he surveyed the two bedraggled women, barefoot with strands of dripping wet hair in place of the usual elegant styling. They were shivering despite the hypothermia wraps covering their soaking clothes.

"Let's get you both into the car and back to your hotel."

"But we have checked out of our hotel and our luggage is in our car at a car park."

"We have already checked you back into the Hera, and if you give me your car keys and parking ticket, we can get your cases delivered for you."

"Do I look as if I had my car keys and the parking ticket with me?" Ayşe asked with an ironic grin.

"Oh, of course not. Does the Commander have keys to your car?"

"He does, but I would be surprised if he has them with him. My keys are either in my handbag at the bottom of Ömar's boat, wherever you have taken that; or they and my handbag are at the bottom of the Aegean Sea. Not very helpful, I know."

"I assume Ömar is the boatman who took you out. Am I right?"

"Yes, he is, and I hope he isn't in too much trouble. He helped save all our lives, you know."

"Leave the problem of your car with me," Djavid said, trying to regain control of the conversation. "The Commander has asked me to take you back to the hotel, give you time to get into warm clothes, have a rest and something to eat."

"We will need our clothes before we can do any of that," Ayşe said, losing patience with her husband's pedantic colleague. "I am sure there must be someone in your cells who can open a car door without the benefit of keys."

"Of course, we'll get your cases to you as soon as possible. I will come to the hotel later this evening with a colleague from Izmir police to take an initial statement from both of you."

"I look forward to it. And are we likely to see our husbands any time soon?"

"That I cannot tell you, Ma'am. They have much to do this evening, but I am sure they will be anxious to see you as soon as possible."

The whole exchange had been in Turkish so Anya was in the dark about what was happening as they were led to the waiting police car. She had picked up on Ayşe's exasperation with the detective and with whatever instructions he had passed on—instructions she was sure would have come straight from their husbands.

Back in their old room at the Hera, warm baths, thick towelling robes and two large glasses of wine did much to restore their spirits. They should have been exhausted, but vestiges of the adrenalin which had raced through their bodies earlier in the day meant they felt remarkably alert.

Following a sharp knock on the door, two men came barrelling into their bedroom and both women experienced the novel sensation of being simultaneously hugged and berated by furious, angrily relieved husbands.

Ayşe lost patience with Kadir's emotional harangue. "I don't know why you are so annoyed. We recognised and followed a man you would have lost if we hadn't spotted him. He would have disappeared by the time the local police got to the car park. Did I mention that he nearly ran Anya over!"

"And would have done if he had known who she was. Have you any idea what kind of man you were chasing?"

"Well, we do now," Anya said in an attempt to placate matters.

The frosty atmosphere became glacial when John and Kadir admitted that they couldn't stay long. The Izmir police had reluctantly agreed to allow Ulrich to be taken back to Istanbul once they were satisfied that he had told them everything there was to tell about the kidnap of Miriam Stavlakis, and his reasons for taking her hostage. It had taken a few hours of tough questioning to establish that the kidnap had been opportunistic rather than linked to Nicos Stavlakis's business interests, as first suspected. Miriam Stavlakis was unharmed—physically at least—therefore the charges Ulrich faced in Istanbul took precedence. Kadir and John were heading back to Istanbul to prepare for the interrogation of Ulrich the following morning.

"If my daughters ever tell me they are thinking of marrying policemen, I will lock them in their rooms until they get over it!"

Anya laughed in sympathy at her friend's outburst.

Reunited with their clothes, Anya and Ayşe went for a quick supper before Chief Inspector Djavid and his Izmir colleague arrived to take their statements. It was almost midnight before the police left and, adrenalin long since spent, both women were utterly exhausted and heading for bed when Ayşe was approached by the hotel manager.

"We have changed your room, Madam." Noting annoyance flash across his guest's face, the manager hurried on to add, "Your belongings have been moved to the bridal suite—I trust you will find it to your liking."

"And I trust this will not involve extra costs."

The manager just smiled, "There will be no charge. I think you will find a note in the suite explaining everything."

"Do you think our husbands arranged this?" Anya asked as the lift ascended to the top floor.

"I doubt it!"

The manager opened the door of the bridal suite and the women let out simultaneous gasps of astonishment. The already magnificent lounge was festooned with flowers. A magnum of champagne chilled in a silver ice bucket alongside an ornate tray of delicate pastries.

"You will find a note from Mr Stavlakis on the table," the manager said as he closed the door quietly on his way out.

Dear Mrs Demercol and Mrs Arbuthnot,

I must apologise for my brusque behaviour when we met earlier today. Miriam has told me of the very great courage you displayed in saving her from kidnap and drowning at the hands of a violent man. There are no words to express the extent of my gratitude for saving the life of my beloved wife. In the meantime, I hope you will accept the enclosed invitation to dine tomorrow evening at the Relais Artemisia. A car will call for you at 7 p.m. if that is convenient. I regret that I will be unable to join you as I need to be at home with Miriam while she recovers from her ordeal. However, we would be honoured if you could join us for lunch at our home the following day so that we may convey our heartfelt thanks in person. You are welcome to stay at the Hera as my guests for as long as you please.
Yours in eternal gratitude
Nicos Stavlakis

"Wow!" was all Anya could say when Ayşe translated the letter.

"The Relais Artemisia is said to be the best restaurant in all of Izmir Province, if not in all of Türkiye. I believe it is so expensive that there are no prices on anything—the idea being that if price matters you shouldn't be there."

"Can we accept the invitation?" Anya asked as she surveyed their lavish surroundings. "This suite, the flowers and the champagne must already have cost a king's ransom. What are the rules about police accepting gifts here? Back home, the rules are quite strict."

"Kadir would have declined the invitation, but we are not policewomen, Anya. Besides, we are in so much trouble already, this won't make much difference. I have always wanted to see what the Relais Artemisia is like, and with any luck, interrogating Ulrich will take long enough for the men to have calmed down by the time we see them again."

"Do you think they will ever get around to thanking us?" Anya asked. "After all, if it hadn't been for us, the police and coastguards would have been searching for two bodies in the water instead of capturing a wanted man. Ulrich would have been lounging in a Greek bar enjoying his first ouzo as the sun went down—just another holidaymaker relaxing after an invigorating swim. If *we* hadn't acted, he would have swanned off into the sunset, an assassin for hire with another two murders to add to his already impressive CV. Because of us, some measure of justice can be offered to his victims' families knowing that he will spend the rest of his life in jail here or in Scotland."

*

Back at the police station, Ulrich, now resplendent in prison uniform, was awaiting prisoner transport back to Istanbul. He had just been through the first of many long and difficult interrogations about his kidnap of the Stavlakis woman and his reasons for it. It had taken hours to convince the Izmir police that he had no idea of who she was or what her husband did. The silent, watchful presence of the detectives from Istanbul and Scotland during questioning had further unnerved him. Had he overplayed his hand in denying all knowledge of the identity of his hostage? Maybe it would have been better to pretend there was more to the hostage-taking than there was—that way he might have been detained in Izmir rather than facing all that was waiting for him in Istanbul and Edinburgh. Maybe he should just have handed himself over to the Greek police in Lesbos. All that was academic now. He knew he was facing the inevitable end to his long career on the wrong side of the law. So much trouble just because Orhan's sister had got the hots for that interfering Turkish doctor back in Scotland.

If laying the blame for his predicament on Yasmin's shoulders was spectacularly unfair, Ulrich was in no mood to acknowledge the uncomfortable truth. He just added his capture to the long list of injustices he felt life had dealt him, starting with a drunken mother who couldn't even give him the name of his father; then Orhan's ingratitude for the many risks he had taken on his behalf, like disposing of a Turkish doctor who had been sticking his nose in matters that didn't concern him; Ronnie Manson's double-dealing over the Romanian girls; and, worst of all, the appearance of his nemesis, John Arbuthnot. The bastard was supposed to have retired!

In a cell nearby, two scared, shivering boatmen sat despondently on hard cots, unsure what the following day would bring. They had faced hours of questioning about how and when they had met Ulrich and Mrs Stavlakis; why they had accepted the fares when it must have been clear that Mrs

Stavlakis did not want to board the boat; what part, if any, had Mehmet played in the attempted murder of Mrs Stavlakis; and the inevitable questions about why they were operating without a licence or proper documentation. At the end of the interview, the policeman from Izmir told them they would be held in custody until he had decided what to do with them. They had no idea whether their plea to let their mother know what had happened would be heeded or not. It was a sleepless night.

The cell door opened late the next morning and an elderly policeman they hadn't seen before told them they were free to go. Their boats would be impounded until they were licensed, safety checked, and their business properly regulated.

Ömar groaned. Although it was better than the massive fine they had expected, it was a blow. Where would they ever find the money to put their business in order? It took a moment or two for Ömar to realise that the policeman was still talking.

"You have an appointment at Stavlakis Shipping at 3 p.m. tomorrow to discuss the offer of employment." The policeman's tone was almost fatherly. "You'll be starting at the bottom of the ladder, of course, lads, but if you keep your heads down and work hard, this could be the making of you. I have been asked to give you this envelope. It contains bus tickets to Izmir and some money for refreshments on the journey."

The boatmen stared at each other in amazement as the reality of what was on offer dawned. The chance of full-time work and regular pay—an unbelievable dream for young men like them.

Chapter 28
Yasmin

"Where did we go wrong, Mr Arbuthnot?"

John looked across the table at Yasmin's father, who seemed to have aged ten years since he last saw him. They had met at John and Anya's favourite café near Top Kapi Palace to say 'goodbye' before Yasmin and her father returned to Scotland. Mr Cilic was on the verge of tears, his coffee and baklava untouched.

"I don't think you did anything wrong, Mr Cilic. I think Orhan managed to do that all by himself. And you have this wonderful, brave daughter to be proud of."

Yasmin's father's expression softened for a moment as he turned to smile at her.

"You are quite sure you do not want to see Orhan before you leave?" John asked and watched a momentary flicker of indecision cross Mr Cilic's face. Yasmin stiffened, all colour draining from her face. Everyone around the table knew that this would be a decision which would haunt Mr Cilic for the rest of his life. If not now, it was unlikely that he would ever see his son again.

"No. I have no wish to see him. My son is dead to me."

"Have you decided what you are going to do when you get back home, Yasmin?" Anya asked in an attempt to break the awkward silence that followed. "Will you go back to working in the restaurant?"

"I will always try to help my parents as much as I can, but I have decided to go to college. It is a while since I left school and I want to brush up my qualifications so that I can go to university to study criminology. I would like to become a detective one day."

"There are lots of interesting careers you can follow with a degree in criminology, Yasmin. I'm not sure being a detective is the best one for a young woman."

"That is an incredibly sexist remark, John Arbuthnot!" Anya said, a half-smile softening the words.

John looked embarrassed. "It has nothing to do with ability. Some of the very best detectives are women, but it all depends on what else Yasmin might want to do with her life. Long and unpredictable hours make it almost impossible to keep up with social and family commitments. That is all I meant. You know what it was like while I was Acting Superintendent during Markham's long illness. We hardly saw each other."

Before John tangled himself up in further attempts to convince Yasmin that he wasn't an unreconstructed Neanderthal, Anya turned to Mr Cilic, "Will you be going straight back to work, Mr Cilic? I expect you will want to re-open the restaurant as soon as possible."

"For the time being, Mrs Arbuthnot, but I don't know how many people will want to eat in a restaurant owned by the family of a murdering child trafficker! Nor do I imagine many people would want to buy the business for that very same reason. As you people say—mud sticks. Our future is very uncertain, and I am glad Yasmin has decided to move on."

As they waved father and daughter off in a taxi to the airport, Anya turned to John, "That poor family. I wonder if they will ever get over this."

"The parents may not. As Yasmin's father says, mud sticks. At least it will for a while. I have faith in Yasmin, though. I am sure she will do well given the extraordinary courage and determination she has already shown."

"Do you think she could ever become a detective, given that she is the sister of Orhan Cilic, and lived with a drugs gang, however unwillingly, for weeks?"

"I'm not sure. The scrutiny would be very tough and intrusive and there is no certainty that her application would be accepted even if she does come out of the vetting process well. It goes without saying that I would support her in any way I can, but that may not be enough. Anyway, it will be at least five years before she is ready to apply for fast-track entry. Memories may have dimmed by then, and she may decide on a different career altogether by the time she graduates."

"Are the Turkish police completely finished with questioning her?"

"For the time being, yes. She has given a very full statement, but she may be called as a witness at the trial. Much will depend on what Orhan says and whether he pleads guilty or not to all charges. She has given me a separate statement about what she knew about Hafez and his movements on the night of her party; and what she knew of Orhan's business dealings in Scotland. However, DI

McAllister will want to interview her on her return, poor girl. She must be wondering if this nightmare will ever end."

Chapter 29
Cappadocia, Türkiye
July 1997

Salvaging the last few days of the promised but severely truncated holiday, Anya and Ayşe had joined their husbands in Cappadocia. Lying on an Anatolian plain and gateway to the Taurus Mountains, the vast lunar landscape stretched as far as the eye could see. Over millennia, erosion had moulded volcanic rock into cones and towers and carved out deep caves providing shelter and refuge to people fleeing armies and plague, exile and persecution from time immemorial. The four friends spent a day exploring cave dwellings, and the vast complex of underground tunnels and buried cities—a testament to the long history of Anatolia. Neolithic pottery and tools had been found on the site as had the later traces of Assyrian and Hittite occupation.

A sixth-century BCE Zoroastrian temple cut into the rock bore witness to Persian presence, and magnificent Christian churches to the later Byzantine period. One of Alexander's generals had briefly held the area before ceding it to the Romans, followed by Byzantines, Seljuk Turks, Ottomans and finally the modern Republic of Türkiye.

"Where is Anya?" Kadir asked realising that only three of them had reached the summit of a long rise of cave dwellings. They all stopped to look backwards and saw her sitting on a low stone staring at the caves dotted up the rock facade.

"She's just doing what she always does in places with an interesting history. She will be imagining the ordinary men and women who once lived and died here."

"That could take some time in this place!" Ayşe commented.

John was right. Anya was transfixed, seeing in her mind's eye the Neolithic people who had inhabited this space long before the ardent followers of Abraham, Zoroaster, Jesus or Mohamed had left their marks on this timeless land. She saw women clad in skins, clay beads around their necks; children playing a game with stones in the sandy soil; and from later periods, men in tunics and women swathed in brightly coloured fabrics. She heard the sounds of war—screams and clashing metal. Pulling out of her reverie, she looked at the low scrub and occasional olive trees in the surrounding landscape. What had the inhabitants of this place survived on? Perhaps the land had been less arid in the past, allowing for hunting and foraging; perhaps there had once been a lake or a river.

She jumped at the sound of approaching footsteps and saw John coming towards her.

"At it again?" He said with a broad smile on his face.

Rejoining the others she apologised, "Daydreaming again—sorry."

Exhausted but elated after a long and fascinating day, the four had just finished a relaxing dinner in a local restaurant and were waiting to settle the bill.

"What's the joke?" John asked seeing a smile pass between Anya and Ayşe.

"We have something to tell you," Anya replied. "As you are supposed to have retired and Kadir has not had an uninterrupted holiday for years, we have come up with the perfect solution—a holiday to a destination so far away there would be no point in summoning you back no matter what crisis erupts at home." Anya looked over at Ayşe inviting her to continue.

"While we were waiting for you in Izmir, we called a travel agent and booked a four-week holiday to Australia and New Zealand. We leave on the first of December! Kadir and I will leave from Istanbul and you and Anya from Heathrow. We meet for a two-day stop-over in Singapore before the onward flight to Sydney."

For a moment, the two men looked astounded before bursting out laughing.

Chapter 30
Azienda Ospedaliero-Universitario (University Hospital), Careggi, Florence 2008

"Dr Menotti!"—Lara Menotti turned around to see a nurse she didn't recognise hurrying towards her. "Dr Menotti, I am from the Neurology and Stroke Unit. We have an elderly patient who is very confused following a series of TIAs and who doesn't seem to have any friends or relatives. We think he is speaking Arabic, but we can't find an interpreter. He has an Italian ID card in the name of...let me see," the nurse glanced down at a piece of paper, "Amajgar Yousefi. One of the doctors on the ward said he thinks you speak Arabic...Dr Menotti, are you all right?"

Lara Menotti was far from all right. Her head was spinning and her legs had turned to jelly at the sound of the name, however badly pronounced. For she had been born Leila Yousefi, daughter of Amajgar Yousefi. It couldn't possibly be. She had last seen her father twelve years ago as she was dragged from his arms by traffickers at a grim refugee camp in North Africa. Without a backward glance at the Traumatology Unit where she worked, she followed the nurse along endless corridors and stairways to the Stroke Unit, barely listening to the nurse recounting, "Mr Yousefi appeared to have been in Italy for several years, his occupation given as librarian. He seems to have lost the ability to speak Italian, though—probably because of a stroke. All we can make out is that he seems very agitated about someone called Nina."

Tears streamed down Lara's cheeks as she looked at the emaciated figure in the bed. No longer the powerful, robust figure of her childhood memories, but unmistakably her father. His once piercing blue eyes were clouded by confusion and his hair and beard were white, but there was no mistaking the aquiline nose or the fine scar running along his cheekbone—the result of over-ambitious rock climbing at the age of nine. There was no sign of recognition in his eyes as he gripped Lara's wrist and whispered, "Nina, Nina." Was Nina a wife, a partner? Whoever she was, she was important enough for her father to struggle through the limitations of speech to get a message across. But what was the message? Lara hesitantly switched to Kurdish—a language she hadn't heard or spoken for a decade.

"Babo, it's me, Leila—your daughter Leila."

"Leila is dead—killed!"

"I am not dead, Babo. I was saved by a wonderful priest and the even more wonderful Dr Yilmaz in Siracusa. I was given a new identity and brought up by foster parents in Palermo. I am a doctor now, at this hospital…and I can't believe I have found you."

A thin hand reached up and traced her face, "Is it really you? The voice—the voice, so like my Leila."

Back home that evening, Lara watched as Nina explored her new territory and new mistress. To say the least, Nina had a richly diverse genetic heritage. She was the size of a springer spaniel but there all similarity ended. Her coat was largely brown with random patches of white here and there. Rebellious ears surmounted a gentle face, and at the other end, a large tail threatened instant destruction to all low-lying objects. Nina would be resident until her owner was well enough to come home. The discovery of his daughter and knowing that his beloved dog was in good hands were doing more to speed up Amajgar's recovery than all the otherwise excellent medical care he was receiving.

Lara had long given up hope that her parents, brother, and baby sister might still be alive. She had sensed their loss since her earliest days in Palermo. She had grown to love the Menotti family who had given her a loving home, helped her through the confusion of her teenage years and supported her ambition to become a doctor. She had been grief-stricken when her foster parents told her that Dr Yilmaz had died in Scotland. They didn't know the details, so at the age of eighteen, she traced Daniele Antar, the doctor who had worked with Dr Yilmaz at the Cordari Clinic, to a hospital in Alexandria and persuaded her foster parents to take her to Egypt to meet him.

Daniele lived in a gracious apartment on Alexandria's once fashionable corniche. Although the international jet set had long since shifted its allegiance to the south of France, the area still retained a faded elegance. Daniele lived alone. Over the years, potential partners had been frightened off by the emotional baggage accumulated from working in war zones, from threats to his life and abrupt escape from Siracusa, and the subsequent violent death of Hafez. He lived for his work and once a year took leave from the hospital in Alexandria to spend a month with Médecins Sans Frontières or the Red Crescent in whichever war zone needed a skilled traumatologist most.

He suggested meeting Lara and her foster parents at his apartment. When the taxi drew up, he could hardly believe that the tall, beautiful woman who stepped out of it was little Leila whose life had hung in the balance for days and whose survival was a tribute to Hafez's skill and determination. What Daniele had to tell them about Hafez was devastating and reinforced Lara's determination to become a doctor in his memory. "I owe it to him," was all she said.

During the summer of her third year at medical school, Lara joined Daniele who was working with the Red Crescent in Lebanon and realised that traumatology was what she wanted to do. Someone had fought very hard to save her life and it seemed only right that she should do the same for other critically injured people. Working with the Red Crescent became what she did whenever she had time off from her studies and as her skills and experience increased, Daniele sought her out more and more often.

Despite a twenty-year age difference and geographical distance, they became very close. Lara had no shortage of younger admirers, but the trauma of being ripped from her family, trafficked, and subjected to multiple rape and miscarriage had left its mark and few of the young men she had dated could be expected to understand the impact this inevitably had on her capacity to trust. The men in her year group referred to her as the Ice Maiden.

Chapter 31
Amajgar's Story
Florence 2008

As the effects of the TIA receded, Amajgar's long-term memory returned and with it, the anxiety of just how he would tell his daughter about all that had happened since she was taken from him. Leila grabbed every spare minute she could to be beside him, but she was seldom able to linger for long enough to begin the story, nor was the surrounding bustle of a busy hospital ward the right place to revisit traumatic events long since buried in the interest of day-to-day survival.

"Mama and the little ones didn't make it?" Leila had asked.

"No," the whispered reply. Neither was ready for that conversation and Leila had hugged her father and left seeking the privacy of a ladies' toilet until her tears subsided. She had known in her heart they were dead, but that one quiet word of confirmation was devastating. Somehow, she managed to stumble through the rest of her shift, only vaguely aware of the concerned glances of her colleagues. In the hospital car park, she fumbled in her bag for her phone and called Raffaella Menotti, the whole story tumbling out in a barely coherent flood of words and tears.

Raffaella left a note on the kitchen table for Corrado, her husband, and caught the first flight to Florence. What would the sudden reappearance of her father do to the emotionally fragile young woman she loved as a daughter? She could only hope that it would not unravel all the progress Lara had made since her arrival in their family as a severely traumatised child. Much would depend on what sort of man her father transpired to be. One thing was sure—if he turned out to be trouble, he would have Raffaella Menotti to contend with.

As the time approached for Amajgar's discharge from hospital, Lara was determined that he could not return immediately to his tiny basement flat in San Frediano. It was clean but spartan, below street level at the front, but with a window looking out over a tiny courtyard at the back. The main room comprised a basic kitchen area with a sink, two-burner hob, and a small refrigerator. The rest of the living space was taken up with a large dog bed, a single armchair, and an ancient television. A single bedroom and cramped shower room led off from the main room. It would be some time before he could live on his own again, and there was no space in his flat for anyone else to look after him.

Lara's apartment in Via Romana was slightly larger, but not large enough for four adults—Corrado Menotti having now joined them—plus the frail, elderly man who was still very much an unknown quantity and his dog. Not for the first time, Raffaella had the answer. Her cousin owned a villa in Via Farinata degli Uberti on the south side of town, and as she and her husband were currently in Canada helping their daughter after the birth of her fourth child, the villa was vacant.

Over the next few days, Amajgar's story emerged. Some months after Leila had been taken from them, a fellow Kurd paid for a boat to Italy for himself and Amajgar's family. As his wife and children embarked on the frail craft provided by traffickers, Amajgar was held back and put on a second dinghy. After two days of being tossed around in rain and heavy seas, the first craft capsized tossing its human cargo into the water. To Amajgar's horror, instead of heading toward the stricken vessel to rescue survivors, his boat veered away from the scene—the trafficker in charge knew all too well that desperate survivors clinging to his craft would submerge it too. Some miles off the coast of Lampedusa Island, a motorboat emerged from the fog and came alongside their flimsy craft. The trafficker jumped aboard, leaving the tiller in the hands of one of the refugees.

An Italian coastguard vessel eventually picked them up and they were taken to a secure camp on the island. As the days turned to weeks, all hope that his wife and children might also have been picked up by the coastguard faded. He was on the island of Lampedusa for eighteen months before getting the papers that allowed him onto the Italian mainland. During that time, he had pled with every humanitarian agency on the island for information about his daughter who had been trafficked from a camp in Africa at the age of twelve. He saw helpless compassion in the eyes of everyone he asked. If she had survived the journey across the Mediterranean, she could be anywhere in Europe or beyond. Sadly, there was no shortage of men looking for underage girls for sex, and no shortage of women flung out onto the street when they were past their usefulness in that sick trade.

He couldn't search the world for her, but he could search Italy. For years he had made his way up through the Peninsula. A pattern had formed—casual labour when it could be found; the vendemmia (grape harvest) in early autumn, the olive harvest in late October, citrus fruit picking in the south, gathering chestnuts in the north and when he had enough money, the endless search in places where immigrants hung out and women worked the streets, in the hope that someone might know something about his daughter. After ten years on the road, a severe attack of pneumonia landed him in hospital in Florence. There he befriended a fellow patient who owned a second-hand bookshop and offered him a job sorting out books in the back shop. He had worked there until the day he collapsed with a stroke on his way home.

Lara told him her story too, missing out the rapes, pregnancy and miscarriage. Her father had suffered enough. She said she had become feverish and very sick in the barn where she and the other girls were being held, and that she had been taken out and thrown into a ditch in case she infected the others, ruining their market potential. If her father sensed there was more to the story than that, he said nothing.

Epilogue

At first, Raffaella and Corrado Menotti had been alarmed at the prospect of Lara marrying a man old enough to be her father, not least that her stated reason for doing so had more to do with the practicality of being married if she and Daniele were to continue living and working together in Egypt, rather than any expression of undying love. But as they got to know Daniele better, they came to realise that he had the compassion and insight to deal with their complex, brilliant, conflicted, and beloved adopted daughter.

The wedding was a quiet one. Raffaella had resolutely, if reluctantly, relinquished her long-held dream of seeing Lara in a shimmering bridal gown and veil walking down the aisle on Corrado's arm to an anxiously waiting young bridegroom. She had, however, thrown herself into ensuring that this more modest event would be a celebration to remember. The guest list was small but included all the most important people in the couple's lives—the Antar and Menotti families, Amajgar Yousefi, Hafez Yilmaz's sister Sofia from Istanbul and a few close friends.

Lara wore a simple aquamarine dress in shot silk (a concession to Raffaella who had made her views clear on the unsuitability of Lara's customary attire) with a simple bouquet of white roses (a further concession to Raffaella). The official wedding ceremony took place in the magnificent Sala Rossa in the Palazzo Pretorio in Palermo, followed by a blessing in the local parish church (a major concession to Raffaella).

The reception was held in the beautiful Italianate gardens of the Palazzo delle Meraviglie. The caterer, who could not have looked more scared if he had been facing The Last Judgment (Raffaella's instructions had left little room for deviation and less still for error) almost collapsed with relief as compliments rained down on him. Holding hands with Corrado and Amajgar, Raffaella smiled as she watched the newlyweds walking around the garden laughing and talking to guests. She and Corrado had fulfilled the challenging responsibility they had assumed twelve years earlier. It had not always been easy, but seeing the beautiful, caring, capable woman Lara Yousefi-Menotti-in-Antar had become, she was suffused with happiness.

She noticed the wistful look on Amajgar's face and squeezed his hand—was he seeing the life he once had, the home into which his Leila had been born, grieving the loss of half her childhood, and the absence of her mother, brother and sister on this special day? She could do nothing for pain which was beyond her imagining, but she hoped he found some comfort in the beautiful daughter he had so recently found.